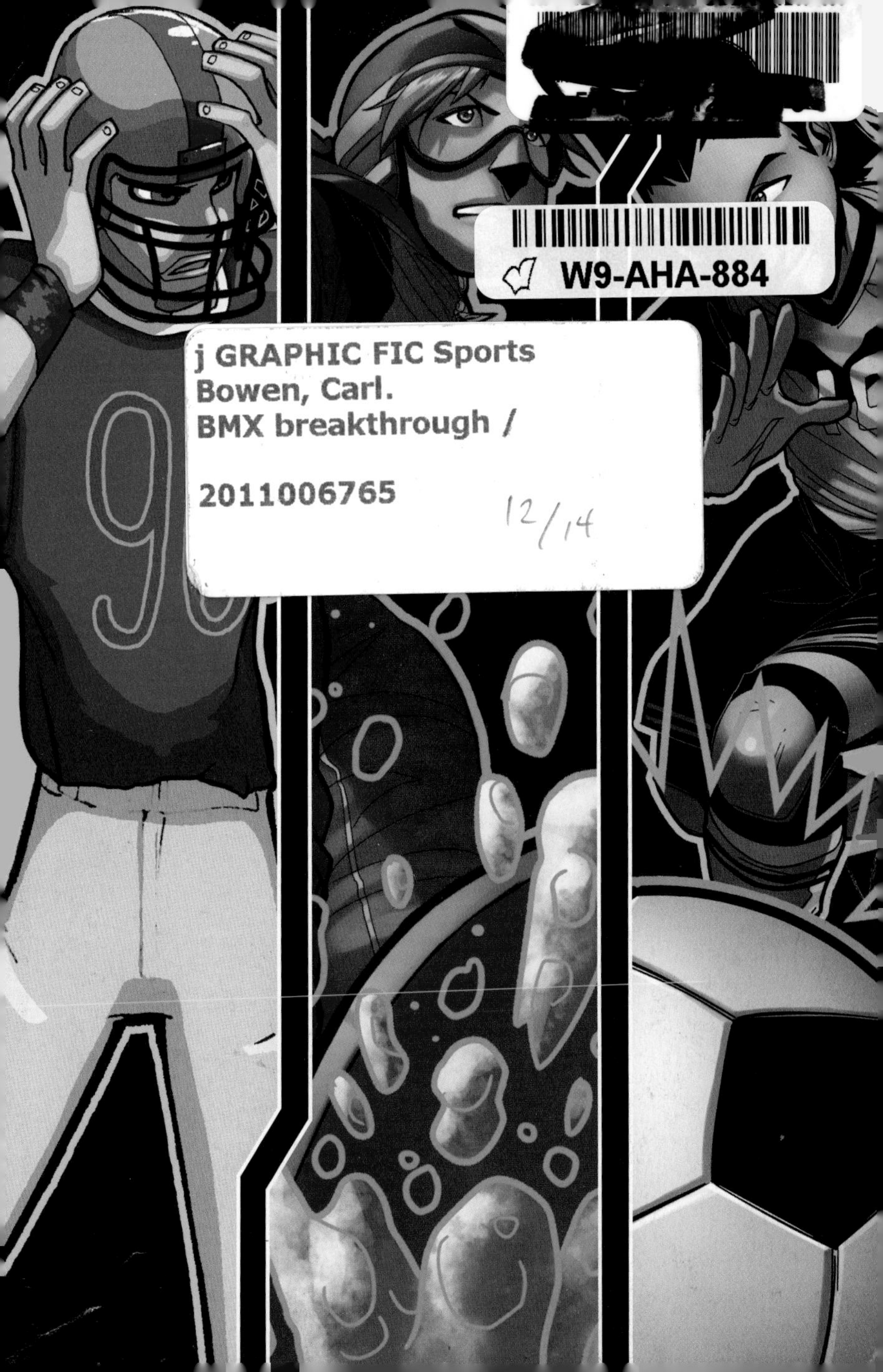

UP NEXT ›››

on Sports Illustrated KIDS

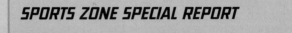

:02 SPORTS ZONE SPECIAL REPORT

:04 FEATURE PRESENTATION:

BMX BREAKTHROUGH

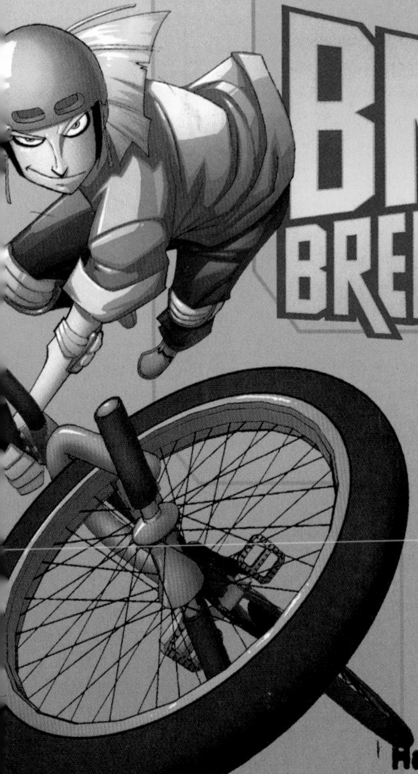

FOLLOWED BY:

:50 SPORTS ZONE POSTGAME RECAP

:51 SPORTS ZONE POSTGAME EXTRA

:52 SI KIDS INFO CENTER

MX TOURNEY WILL ONCE AGAIN BE HELD AT TIDAL WAVE PAR SIK TICKER

BMX
FREESTYLE

BMX BREAKTHROUGH BEGINS!

BILL *CRUZ*

STATS:
AGE: 14

BIO: Bill Cruz is the early favorite to win this year's BMX BREAKTHROUGH freestyle tournament, despite breaking his left arm and left leg at last year's competition. Before going down with the injury, Bill was a lock to win. However, some fans are wondering if Bill will be nervous about facing the same Tidal Wave halfpipe that nearly killed him last year.

PENNY ALLEN

AGE: 15

BIO: Penny and Bill have been hanging out together ever since their bikes had training wheels. But Penny's never been very friendly with Bill or Mike. In fact, she tends to tease them pretty mercilessly — or she did, anyway, until Bill got injured.

MIKE RHODES

AGE: 14
BIO: Mike is one of Bill's best friends. He's always supportive, always upbeat, and tends to see the best in everyone.

MRS. CRUZ

AGE: 43
BIO: She may have the awkward habit of misusing BMX slang, but Bill's mom is a big supporter of her son at his tournaments.

FLOYD EMERSON

AGE: 14
BIO: Floyd doesn't talk much, but this BMX competitor is always near the top of the heap.

WILL BILL CRUZ WILT WHEN HE RIDES THE TIDAL WAVE **SIK** TICKER

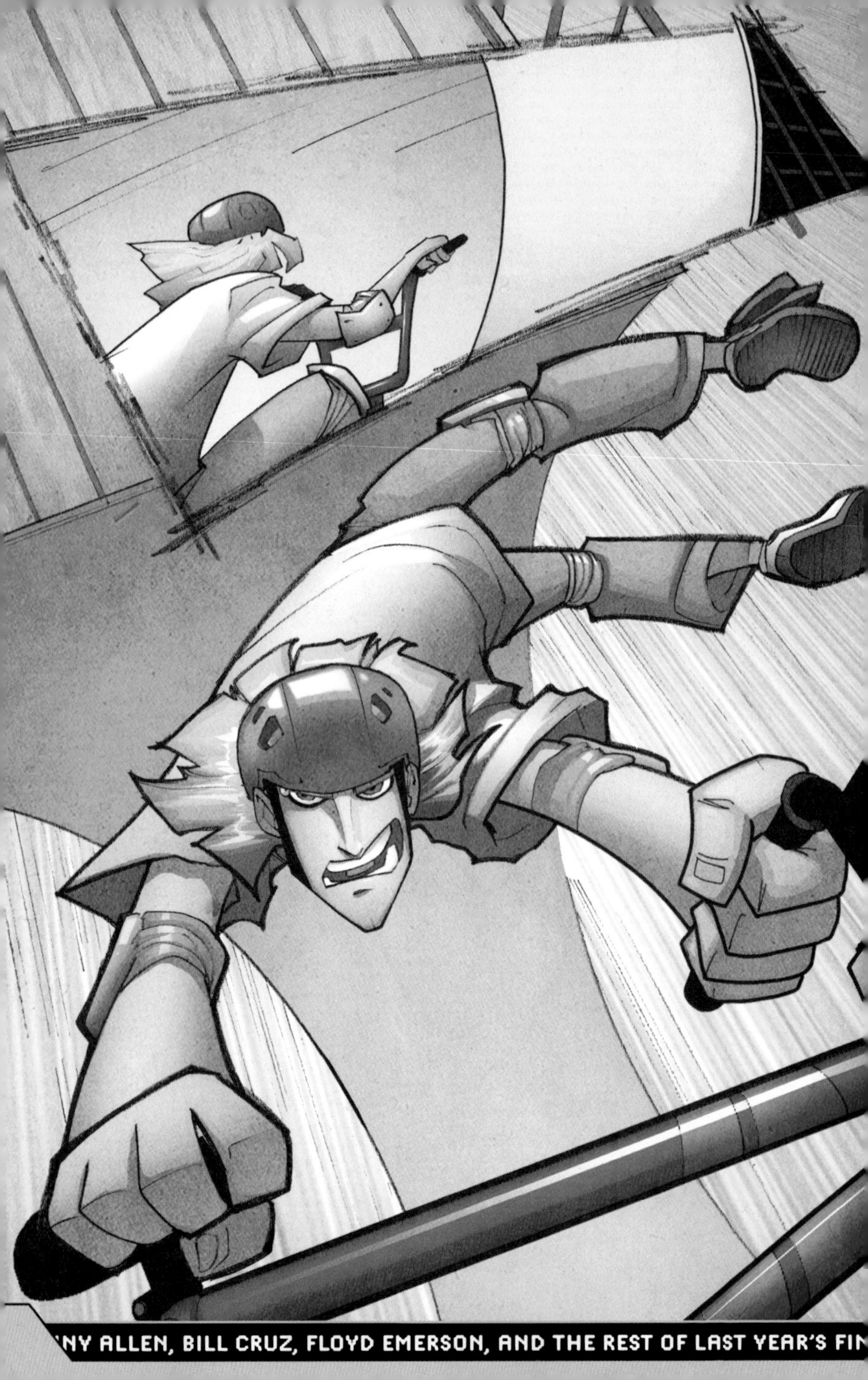
ALLEN, BILL CRUZ, FLOYD EMERSON, AND THE REST OF LAST YEAR'S

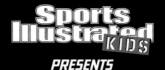

Sports Illustrated KIDS

PRESENTS

BMX BREAKTHROUGH

A PRODUCTION OF

STONE ARCH BOOKS
a capstone imprint

written by Carl Bowen
illustrated by Gerardo Sandoval
colored by Benny Fuentes

designed and directed by Bob Lentz
edited by Sean Tulien
creative direction by Heather Kindseth
editorial management by Donald Lemke
editorial direction by Michael Dahl

Sports Illustrated KIDS *BMX Breakthrough* is published by Stone Arch Books,
1710 Roe Crest Drive, North Mankato, Minnesota 56003.
www.capstonepub.com

Printed in the United States of America in Stevens Point, Wisconsin.
072012 006878R

Summary: After six long weeks of rehabilitation for a broken bone, Bill finally gets back on his bike. But now, he can't help but hold back a bit on his tricks . . .

Library of Congress Cataloging-in-Publication Data
Bowen, Carl.
BMX breakthrough / written by Carl Bowen ; illustrated by Gerardo Sandoval, and Benny Fuentes.
p. cm. -- (Sports illustrated kids graphic novels)
ISBN 978-1-4342-2240-4 (library binding)
ISBN 978-1-4342-3401-8 (paperback)
ISBN 978-1-4342-4941-8 (e-book)
1. Bicycle motocross--Competitions--Comic books, strips, etc. 2. Bicycle motocross--Competitions--Juvenile fiction. 3. Competition (Psychology)--Comic books, strips, etc. 4. Competition (Psychology)--Juvenile fiction. 5. Self-confidence--Comic books, strips, etc. 6. Self-confidence--Juvenile fiction. 7. Graphic novels. I. Sandoval, Gerardo, ill. II. Fuentes, Benny, ill. III. Title. IV. Series: Sports illustrated kids graphic novels.
PZ7.7.B69Bm 2012
741.5'973--dc22 2011006765

RRIVE TODAY TO COMPETE IN THE SEVENTH ANNUAL BMX BREAKT

SIK TICKER

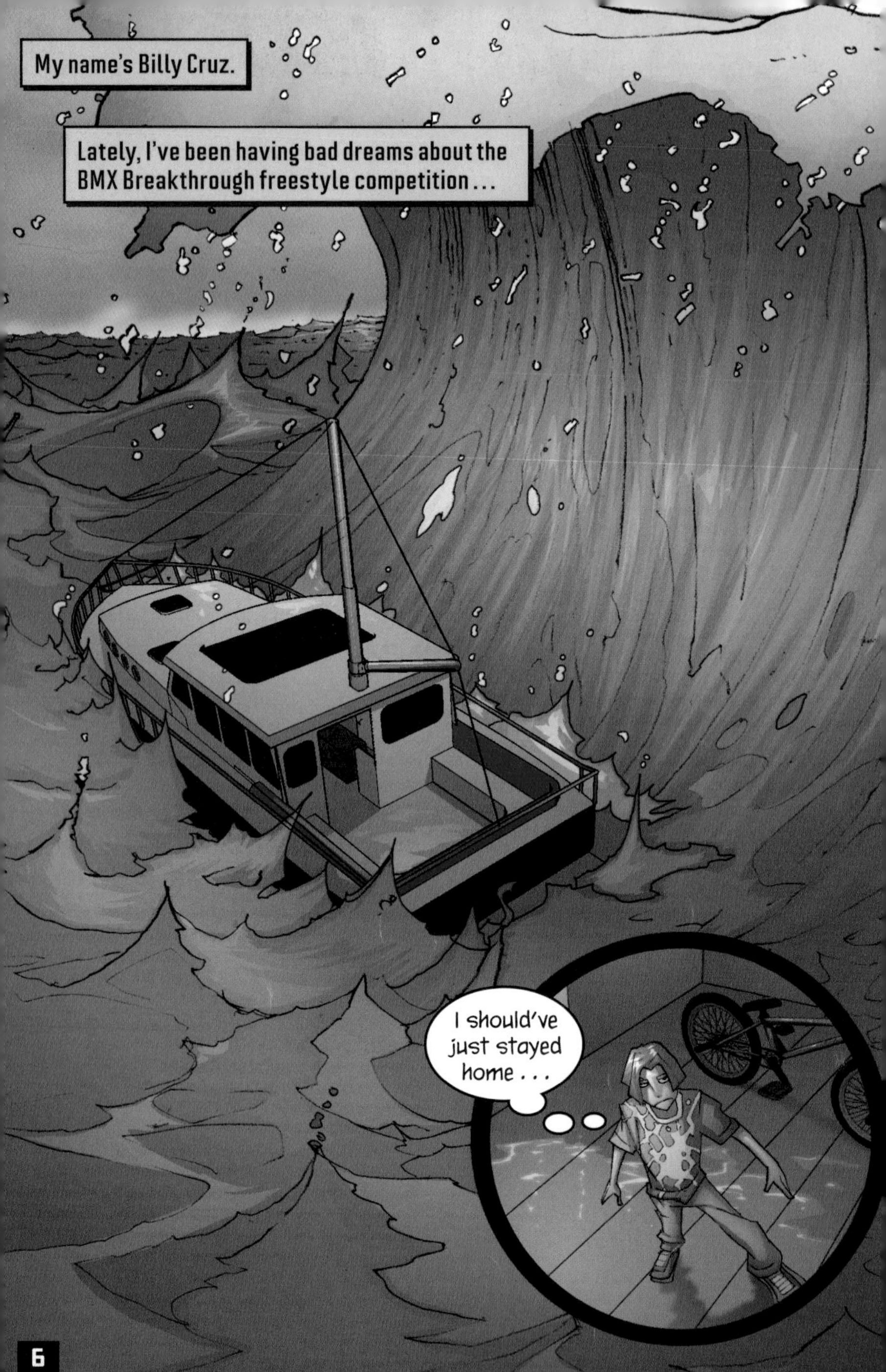
My name's Billy Cruz.
Lately, I've been having bad dreams about the BMX Breakthrough freestyle competition . . .
I should've just stayed home . . .

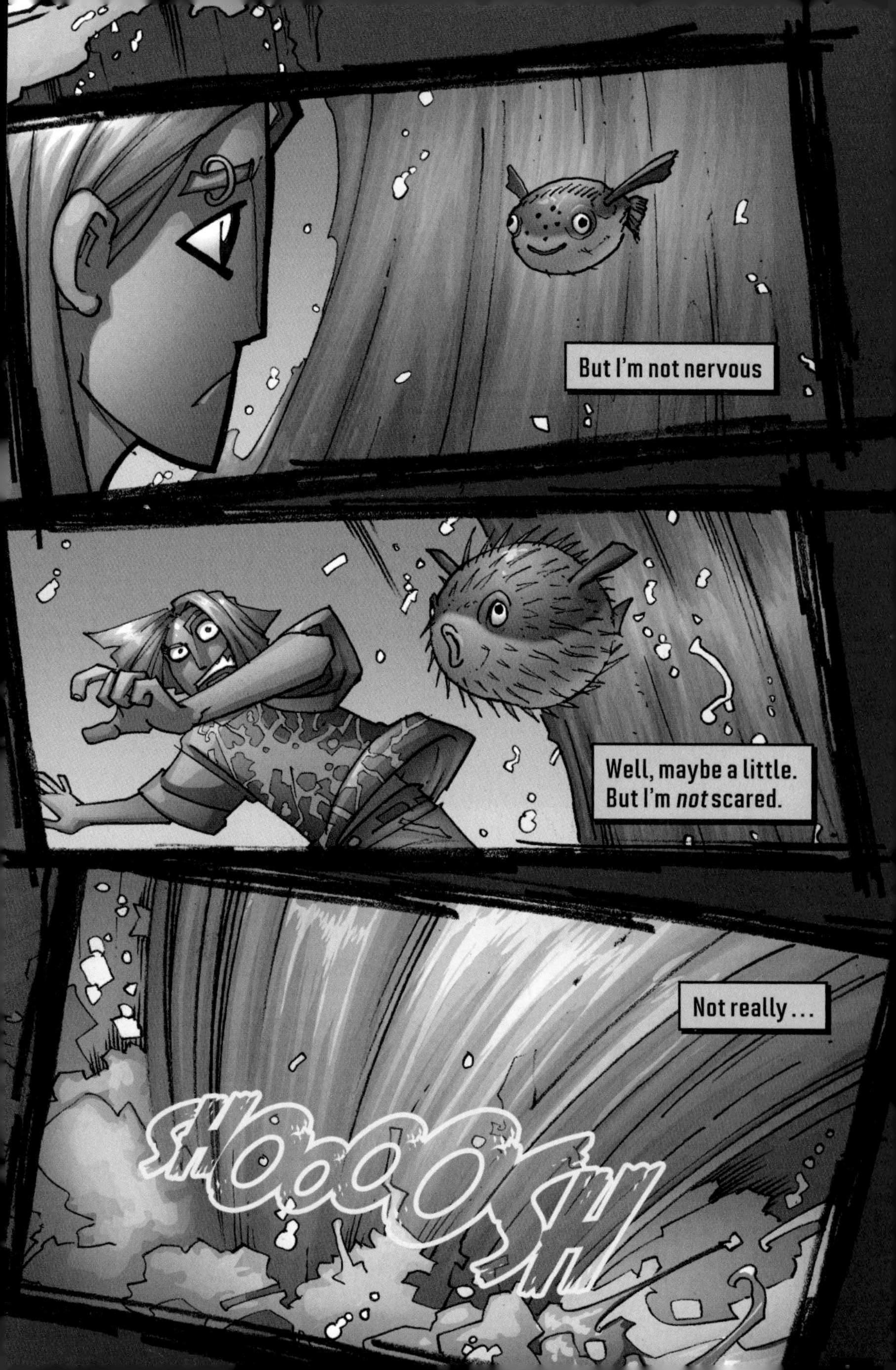
But I'm not nervous
Well, maybe a little.
But I'm *not* scared.
Not really . . .
SHOOOOOSH

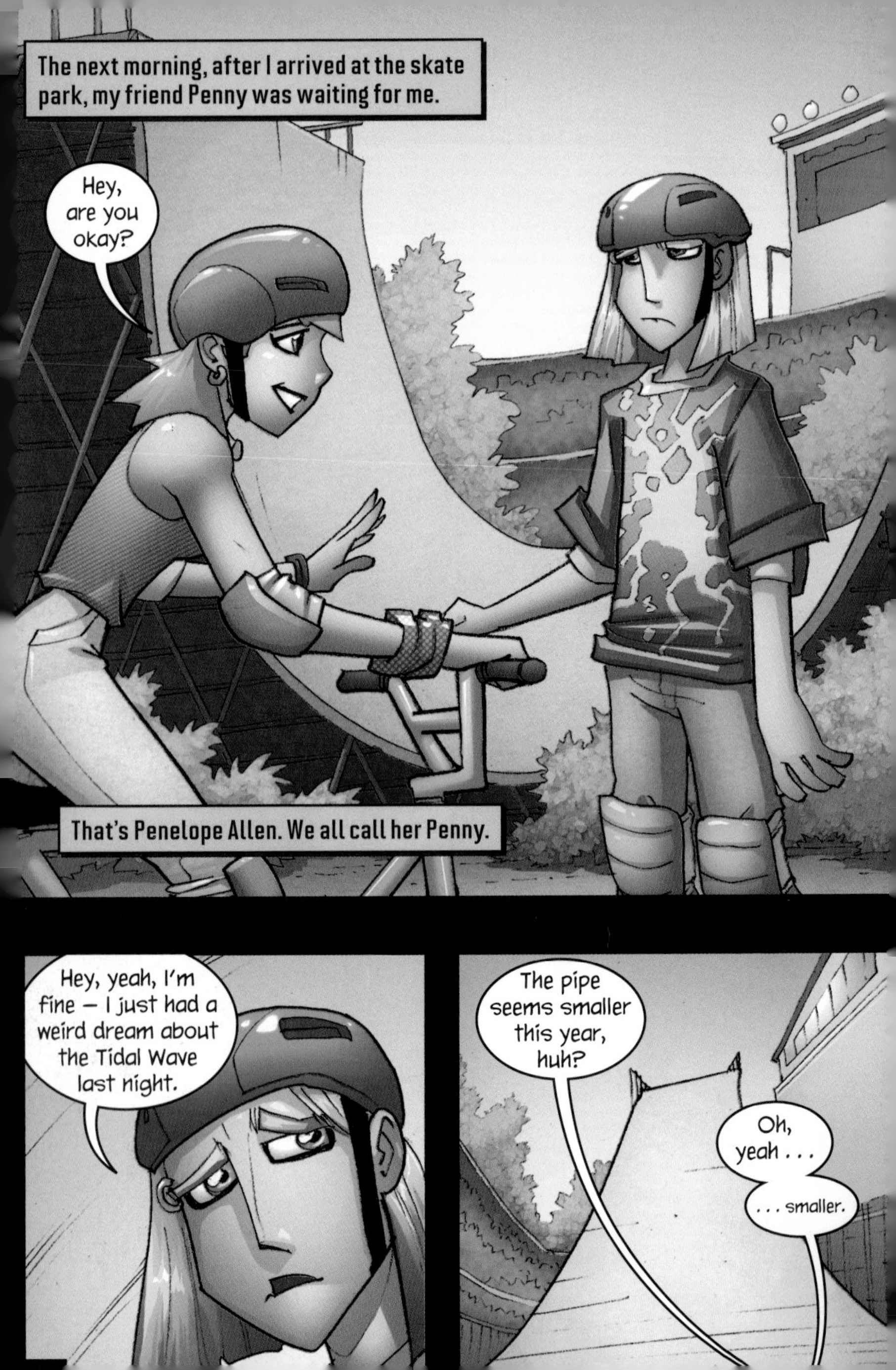
The next morning, after I arrived at the skate park, my friend Penny was waiting for me.
Hey, are you okay?
That's Penelope Allen. We all call her Penny.
Hey, yeah, I'm fine — I just had a weird dream about the Tidal Wave last night.
The pipe seems smaller this year, huh?
Oh, yeah . . .
. . . smaller.

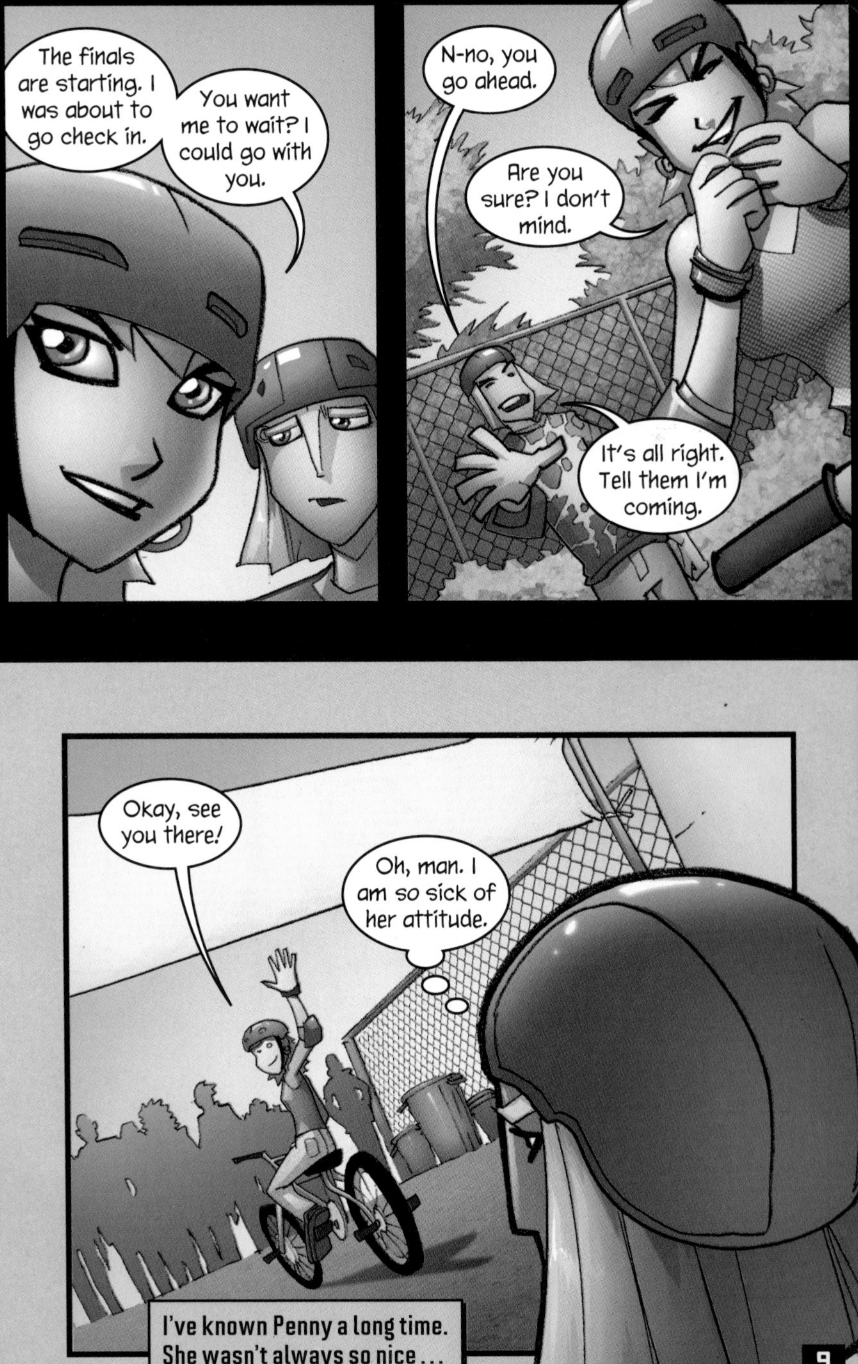
The finals are starting. I was about to go check in.
You want me to wait? I could go with you.
N-no, you go ahead.
Are you sure? I don't mind.
It's all right. Tell them I'm coming.
Okay, see you there!
Oh, man. I am so sick of her attitude.
I've known Penny a long time. She wasn't always so nice . . .

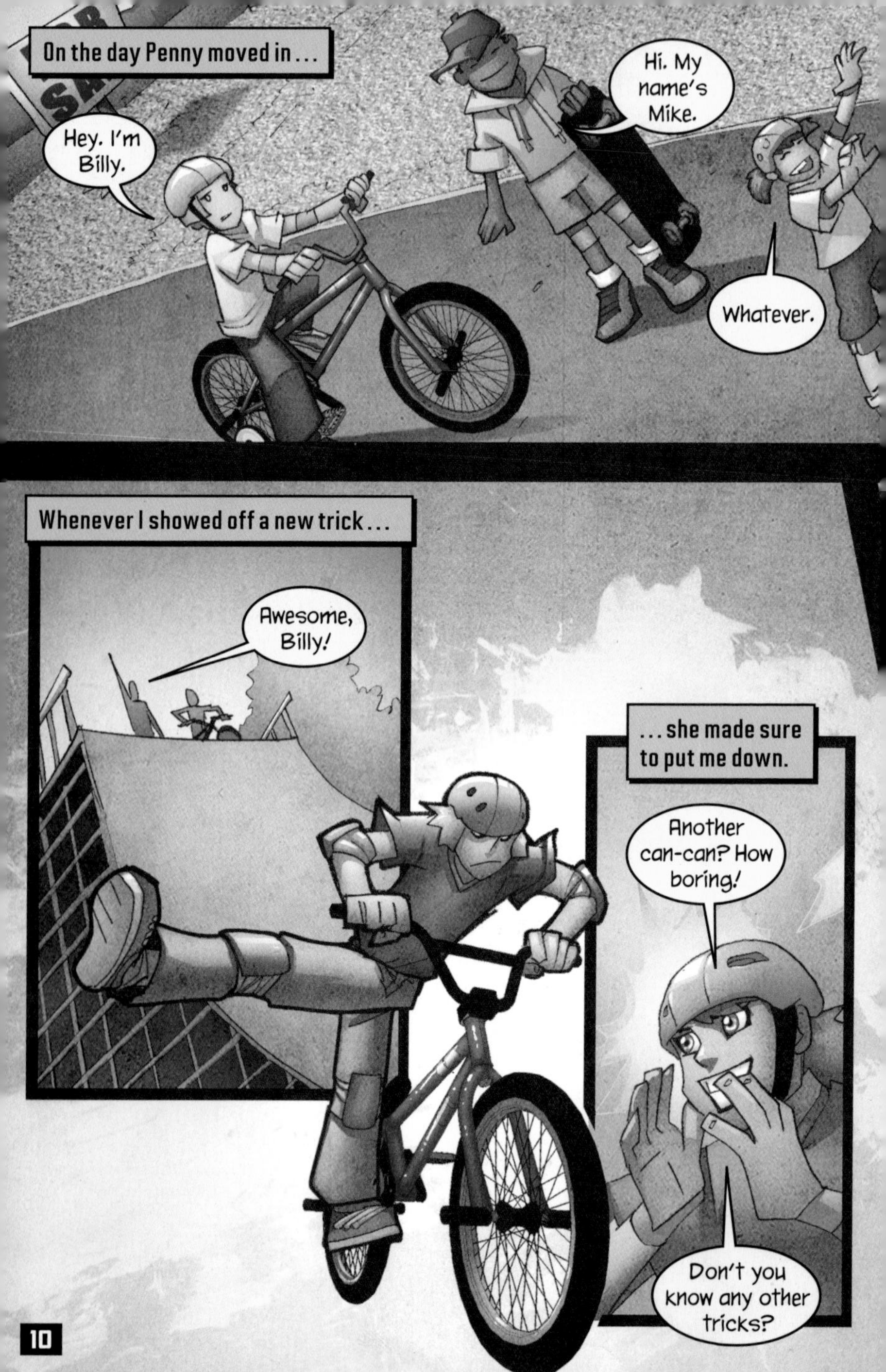
On the day Penny moved in . . .
Hey. I'm Billy.
Hi. My name's Mike.
Whatever.
Whenever I showed off a new trick . . .
Awesome, Billy!
. . . she made sure to put me down.
Another can-can? How boring!
Don't you know any other tricks?

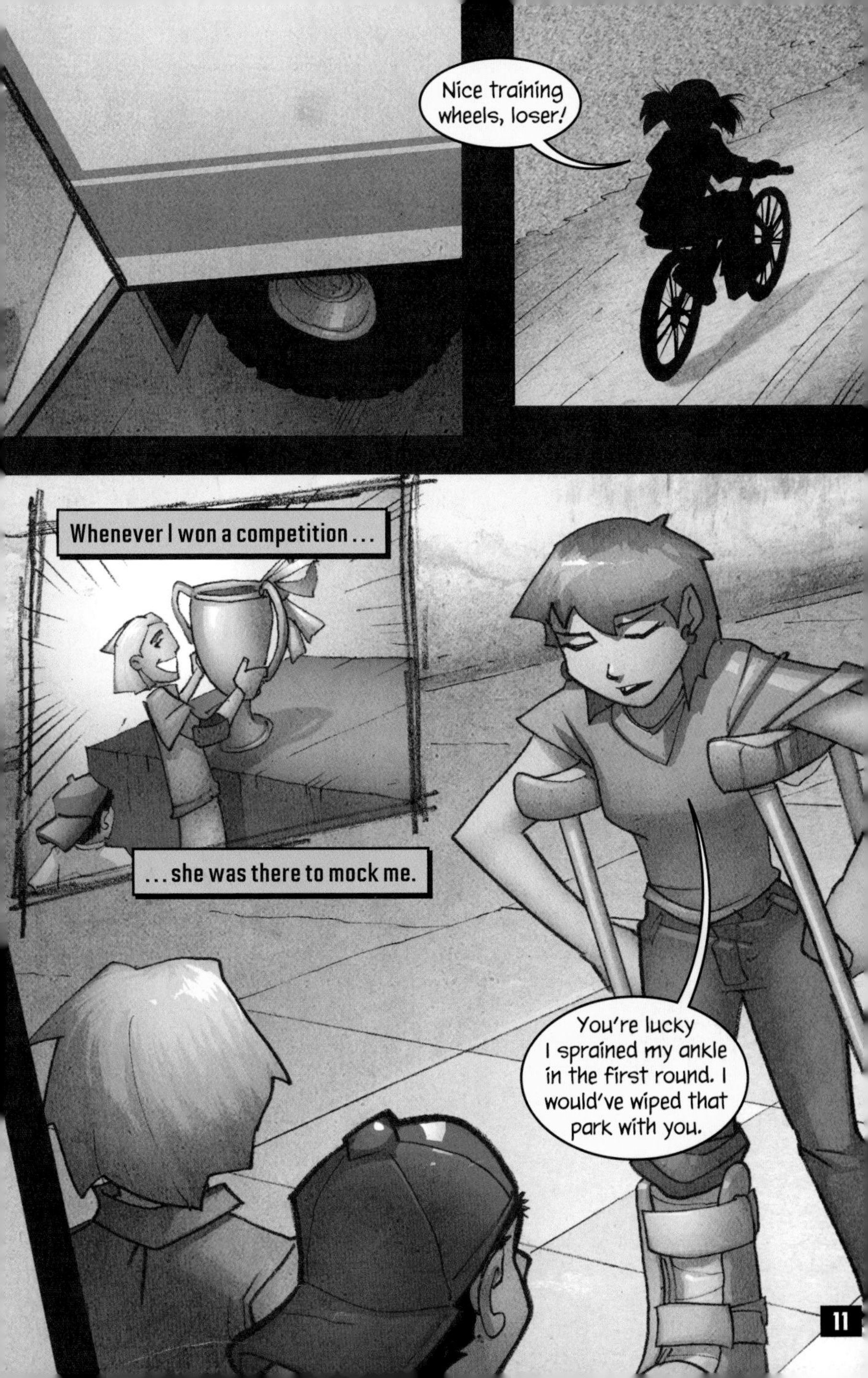
Nice training wheels, loser!
Whenever I won a competition . . .
. . . she was there to mock me.
You're lucky I sprained my ankle in the first round. I would've wiped that park with you.

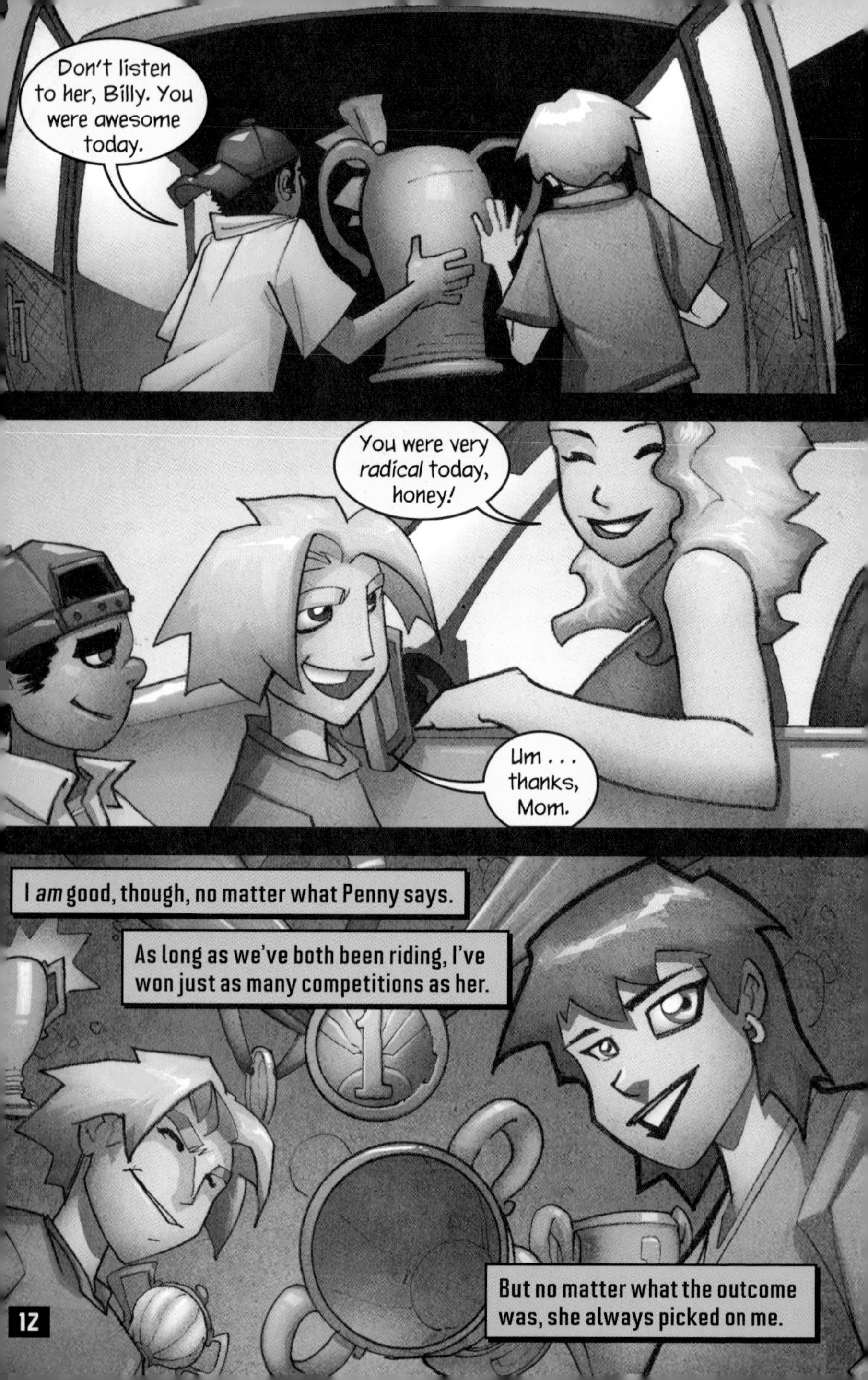

Don't listen to her, Billy. You were awesome today.
You were very *radical* today, honey!
Um . . . thanks, Mom.
I *am* good, though, no matter what Penny says.
As long as we've both been riding, I've won just as many competitions as her.
But no matter what the outcome was, she always picked on me.

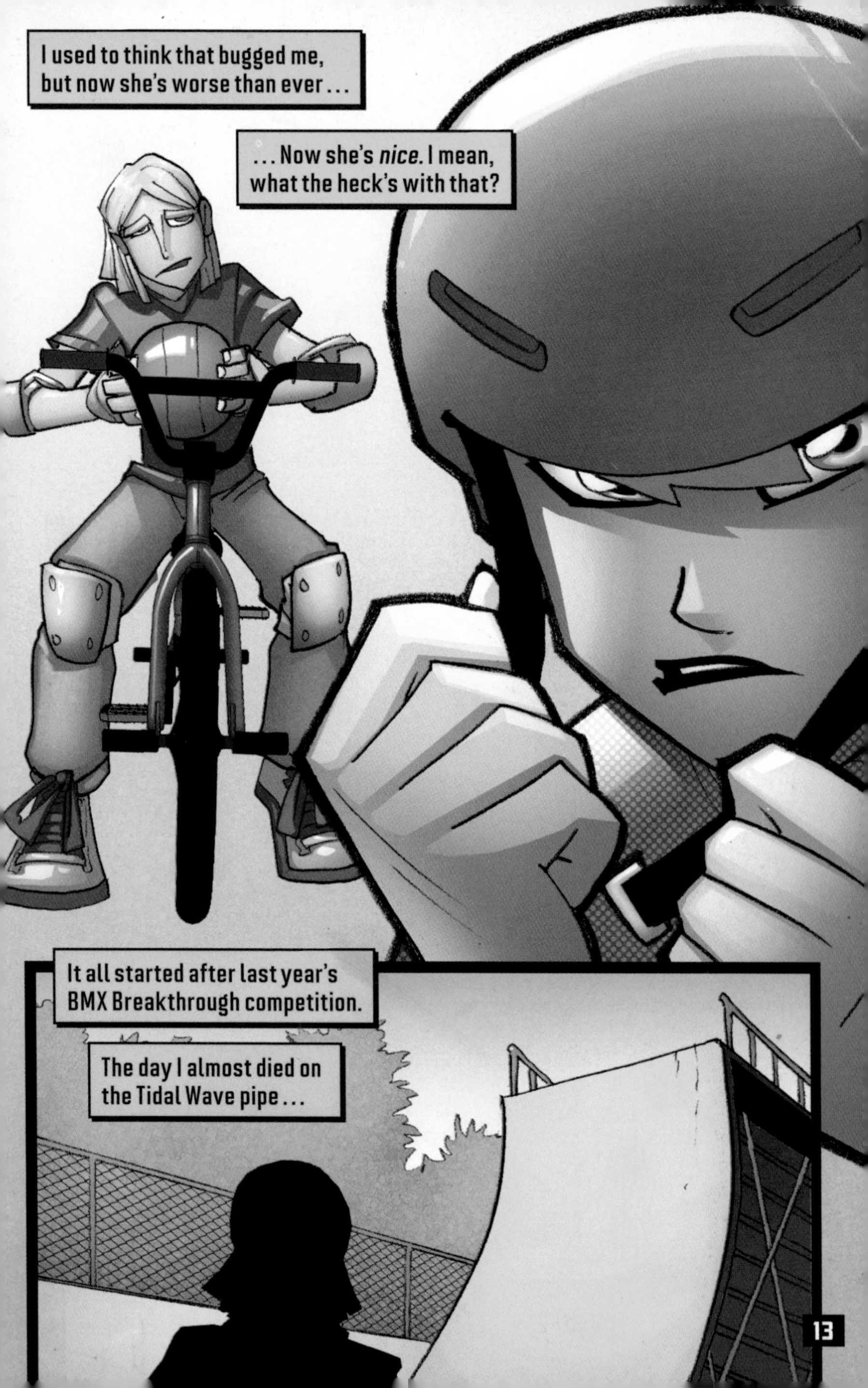
I used to think that bugged me, but now she's worse than ever . . .
. . . Now she's *nice.* I mean, what the heck's with that?
It all started after last year's BMX Breakthrough competition.
The day I almost died on the Tidal Wave pipe . . .

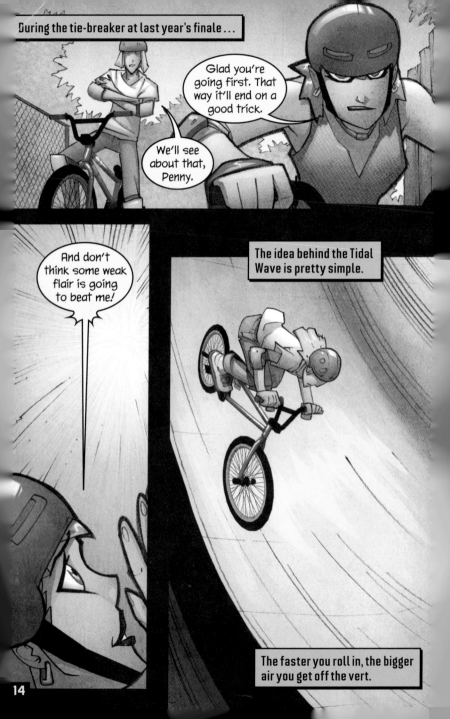

During the tie-breaker at last year's finale ...

Glad you're going first. That way it'll end on a good trick.

We'll see about that, Penny.

And don't think some weak flair is going to beat me!

The idea behind the Tidal Wave is pretty simple.

The faster you roll in, the bigger air you get off the vert.

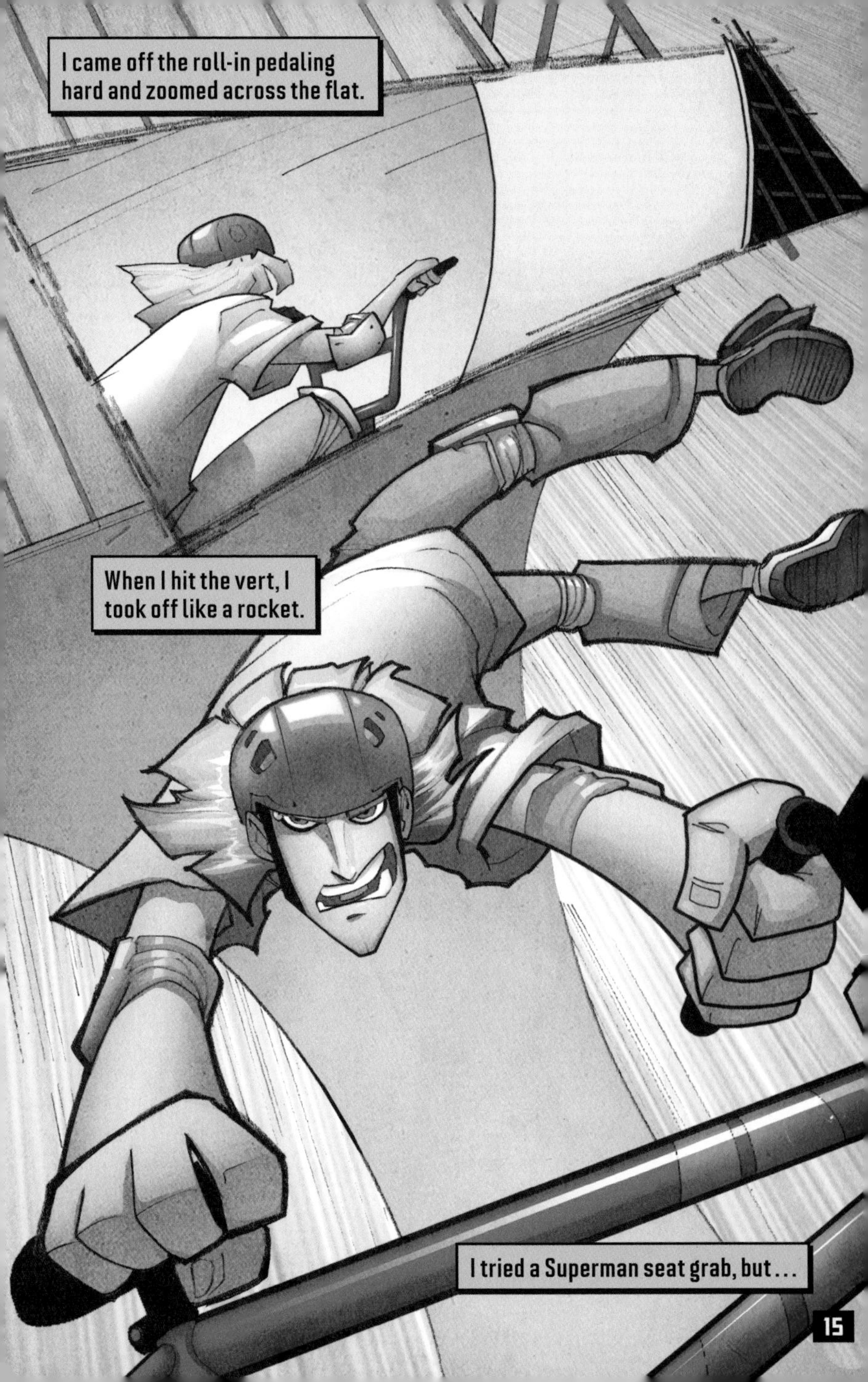
I came off the roll-in pedaling hard and zoomed across the flat.
When I hit the vert, I took off like a rocket.
I tried a Superman seat grab, but . . .

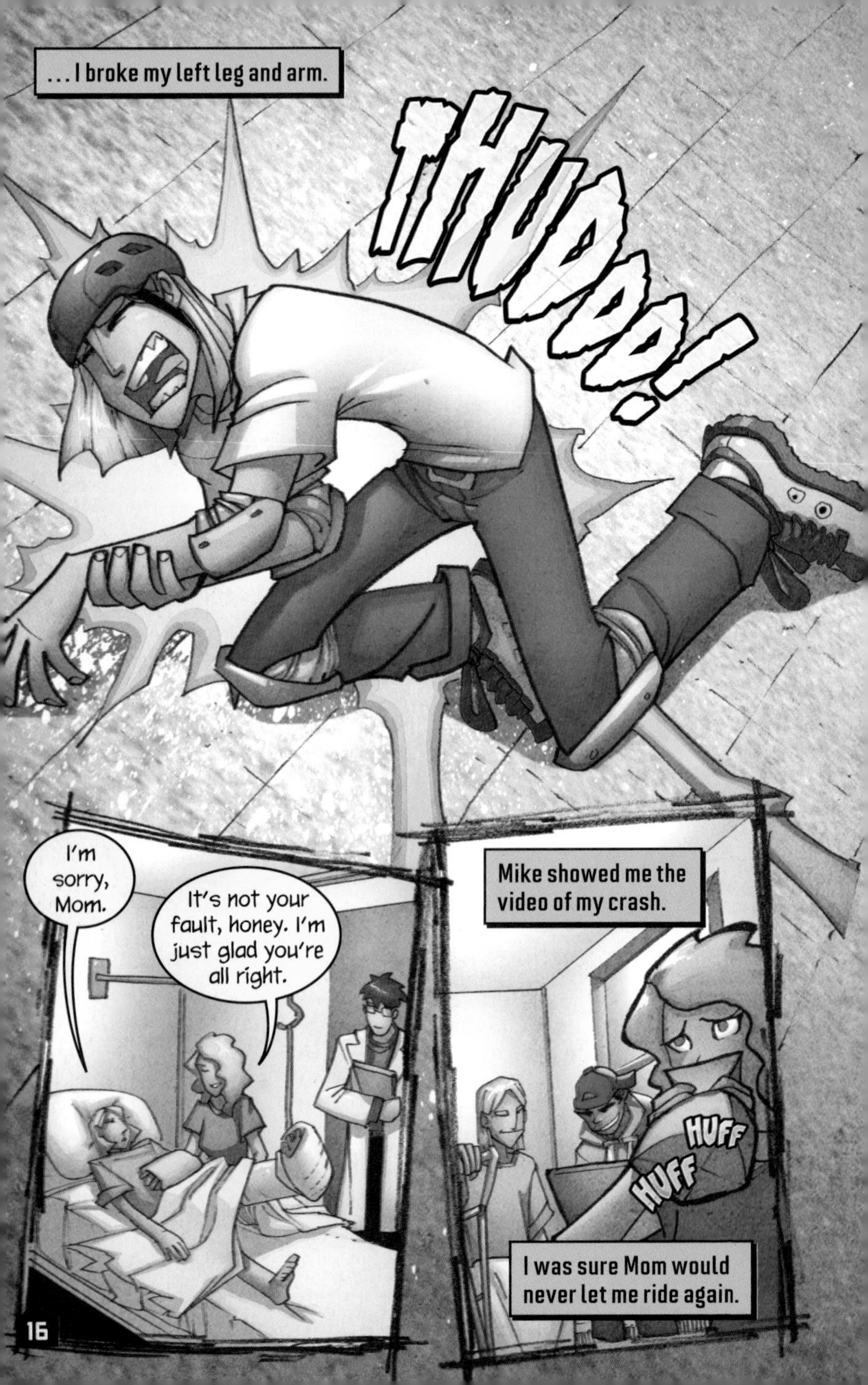
...I broke my left leg and arm.
THUDD!
I'm sorry, Mom.
It's not your fault, honey. I'm just glad you're all right.
Mike showed me the video of my crash.
HUFF
HUFF
I was sure Mom would never let me ride again.

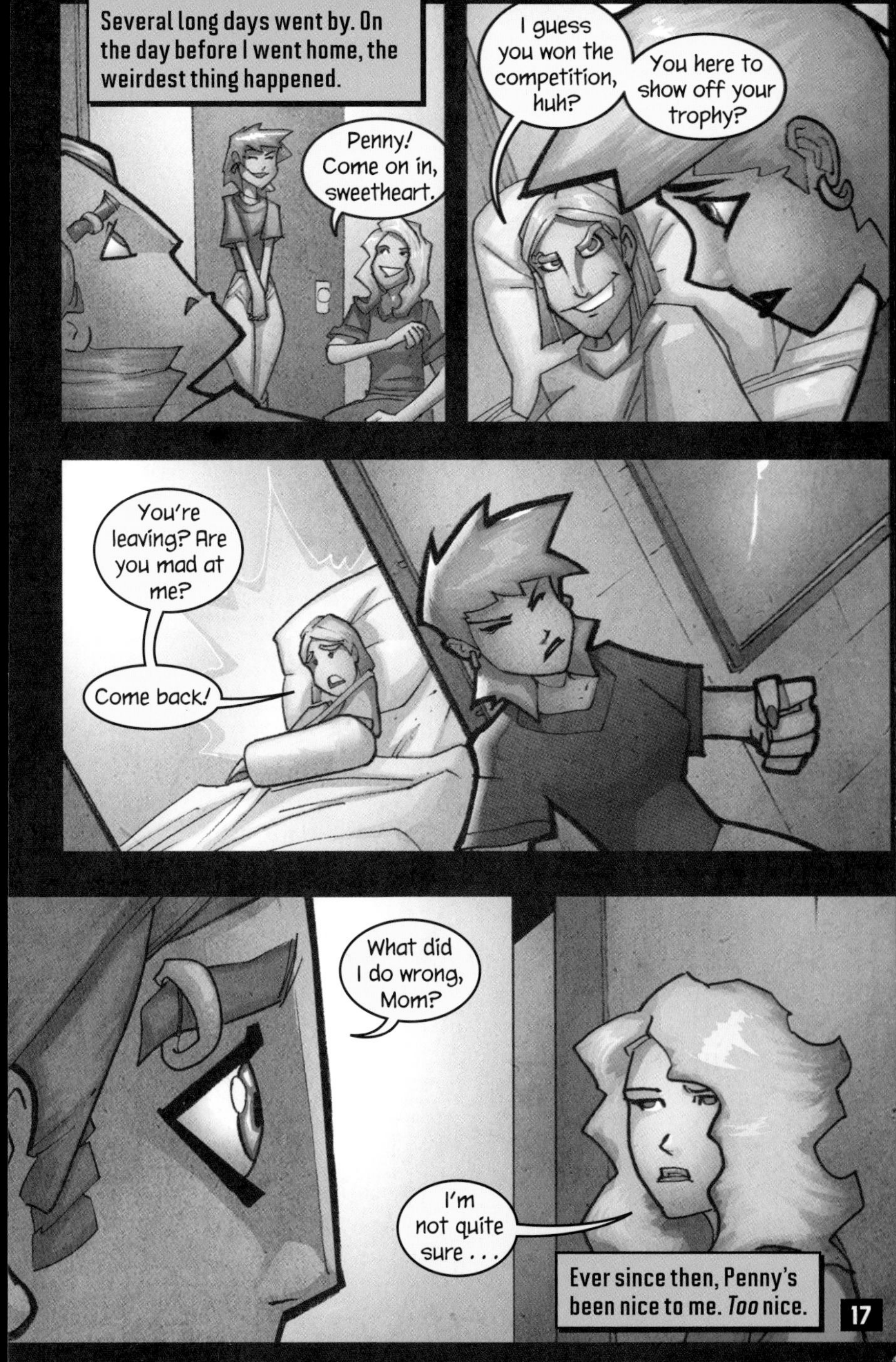

Several long days went by. On the day before I went home, the weirdest thing happened.
Penny! Come on in, sweetheart.
I guess you won the competition, huh?
You here to show off your trophy?
You're leaving? Are you mad at me?
Come back!
What did I do wrong, Mom?
I'm not quite sure . . .
Ever since then, Penny's been nice to me. *Too* nice.

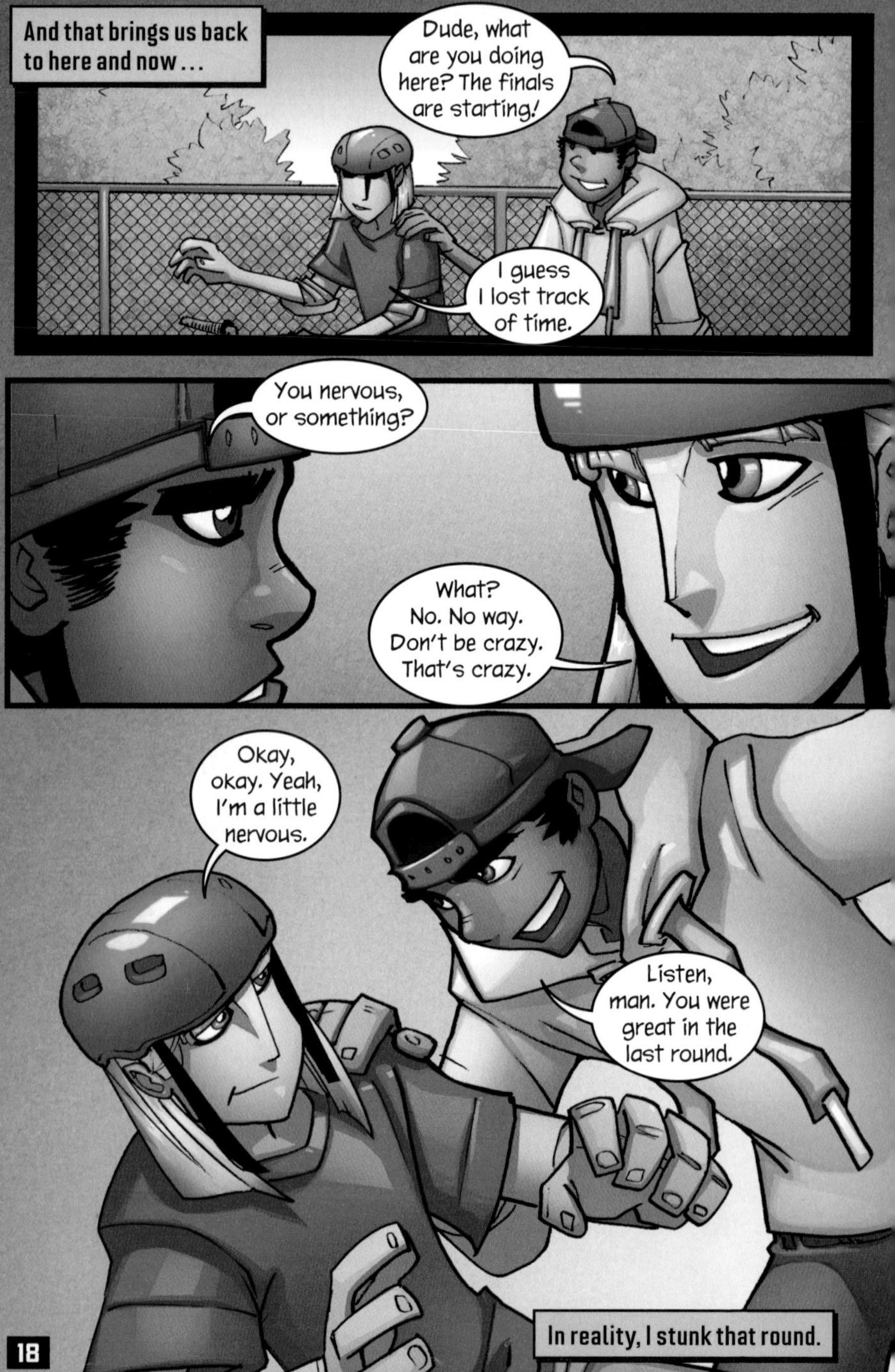

And that brings us back to here and now...
Dude, what are you doing here? The finals are starting!
I guess I lost track of time.
You nervous, or something?
What? No. No way. Don't be crazy. That's crazy.
Okay, okay. Yeah, I'm a little nervous.
Listen, man. You were great in the last round.
In reality, I stunk that round.

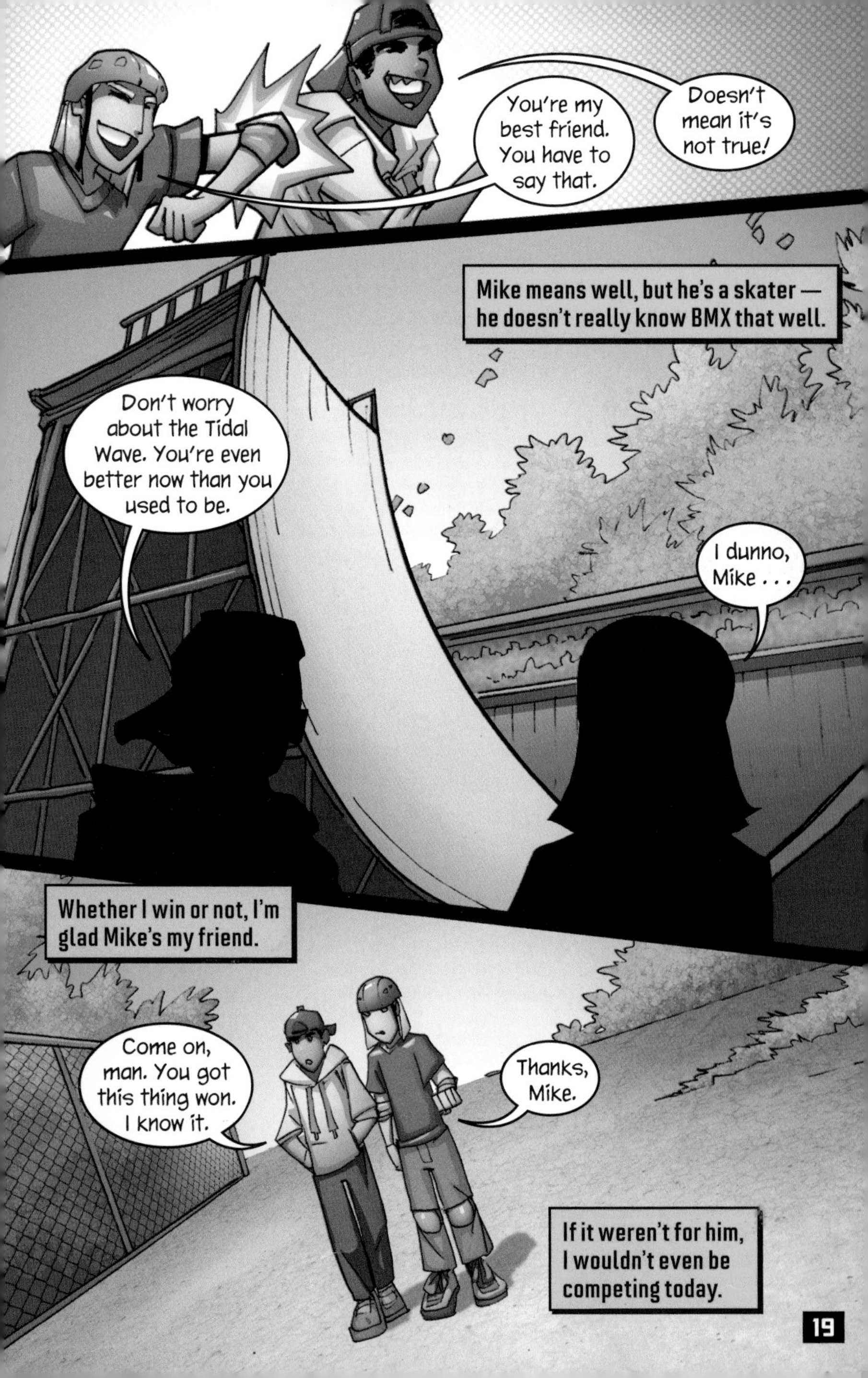
You're my best friend. You have to say that.
Doesn't mean it's not true!
Mike means well, but he's a skater — he doesn't really know BMX that well.
Don't worry about the Tidal Wave. You're even better now than you used to be.
I dunno, Mike . . .
Whether I win or not, I'm glad Mike's my friend.
Come on, man. You got this thing won. I know it.
Thanks, Mike.
If it weren't for him, I wouldn't even be competing today.

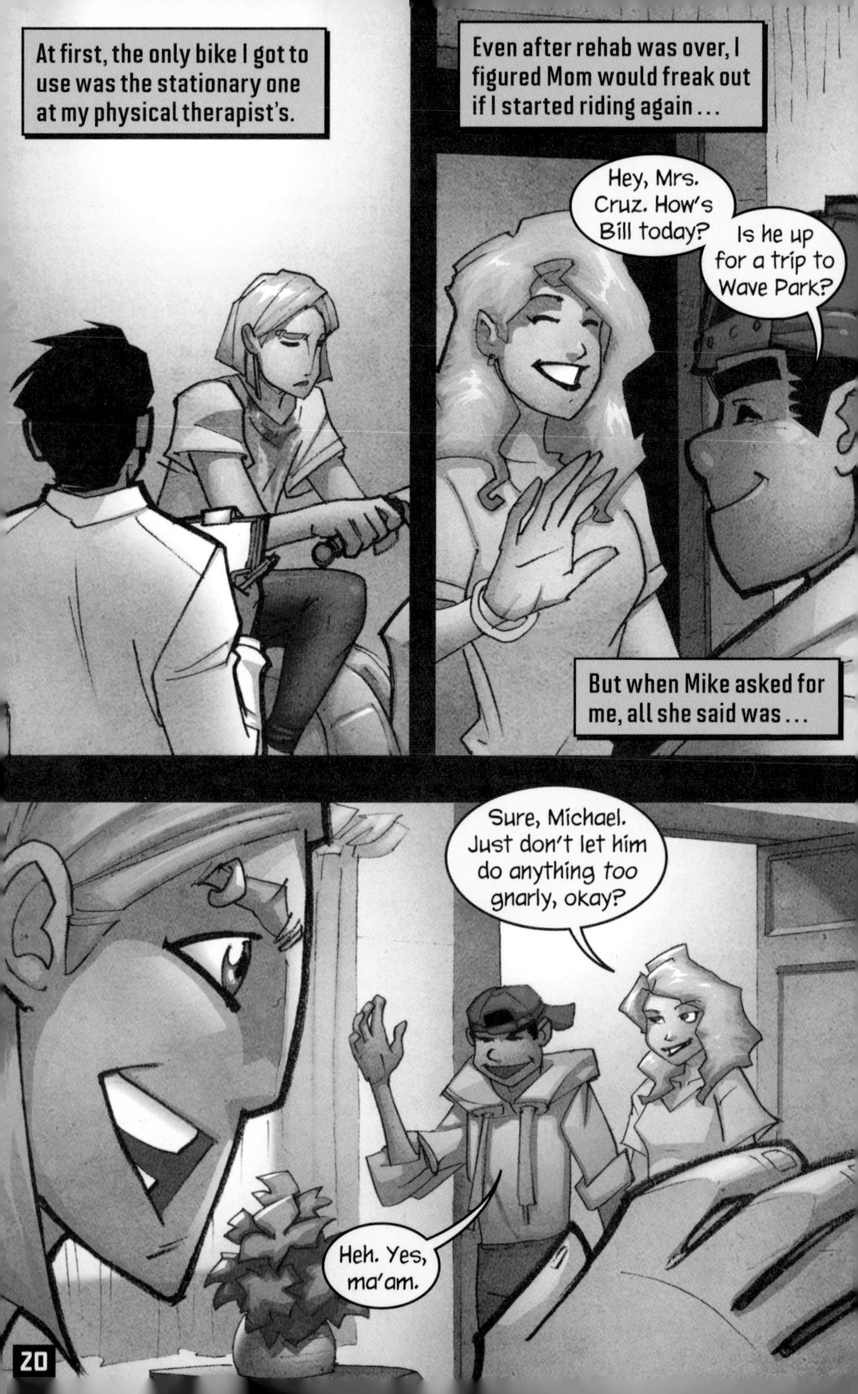
At first, the only bike I got to use was the stationary one at my physical therapist's.
Even after rehab was over, I figured Mom would freak out if I started riding again . . .
Hey, Mrs. Cruz. How's Bill today?
Is he up for a trip to Wave Park?
But when Mike asked for me, all she said was . . .
Sure, Michael. Just don't let him do anything *too* gnarly, okay?
Heh. Yes, ma'am.

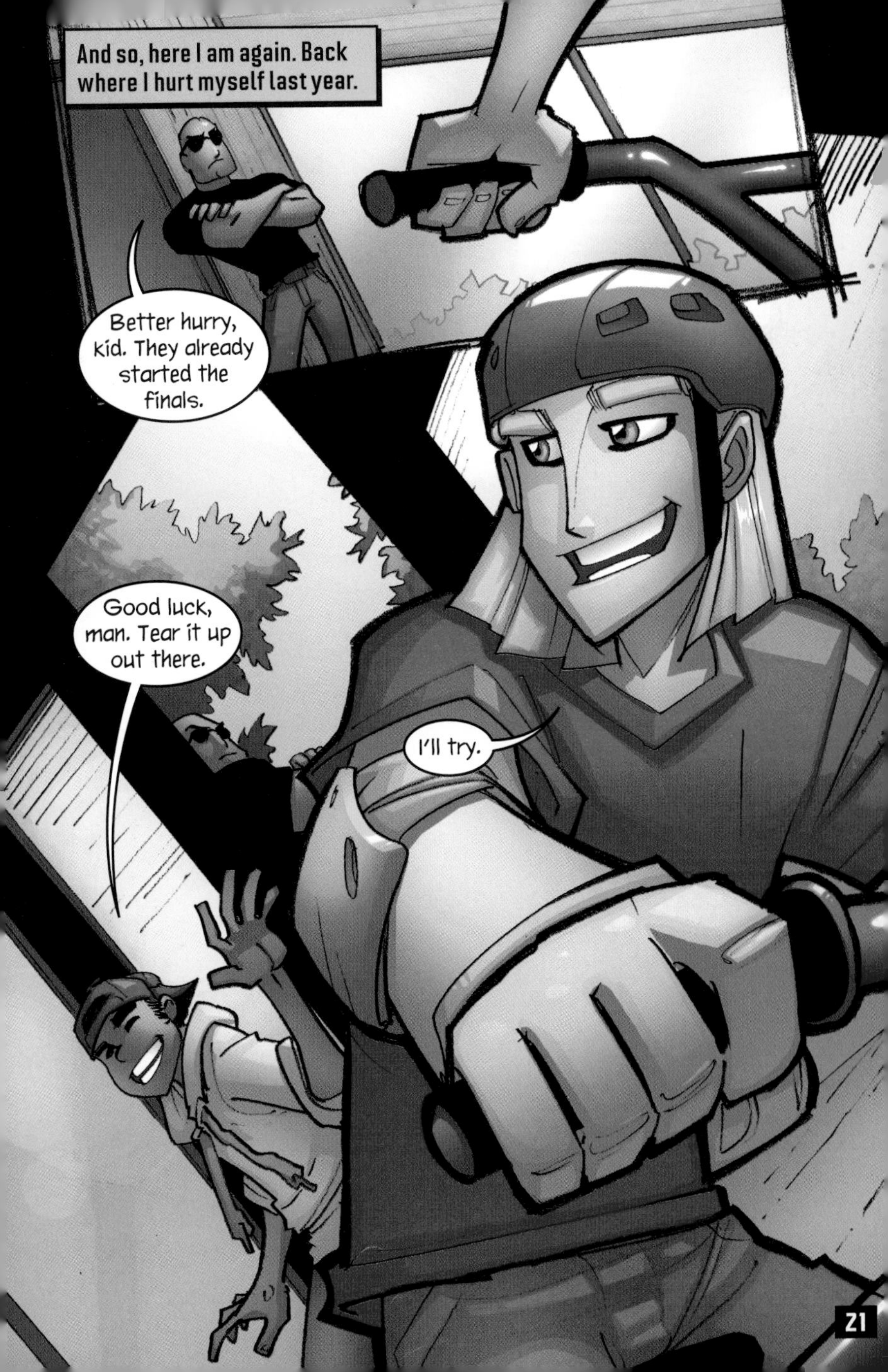

And so, here I am again. Back where I hurt myself last year.
Better hurry, kid. They already started the finals.
Good luck, man. Tear it up out there.
I'll try.

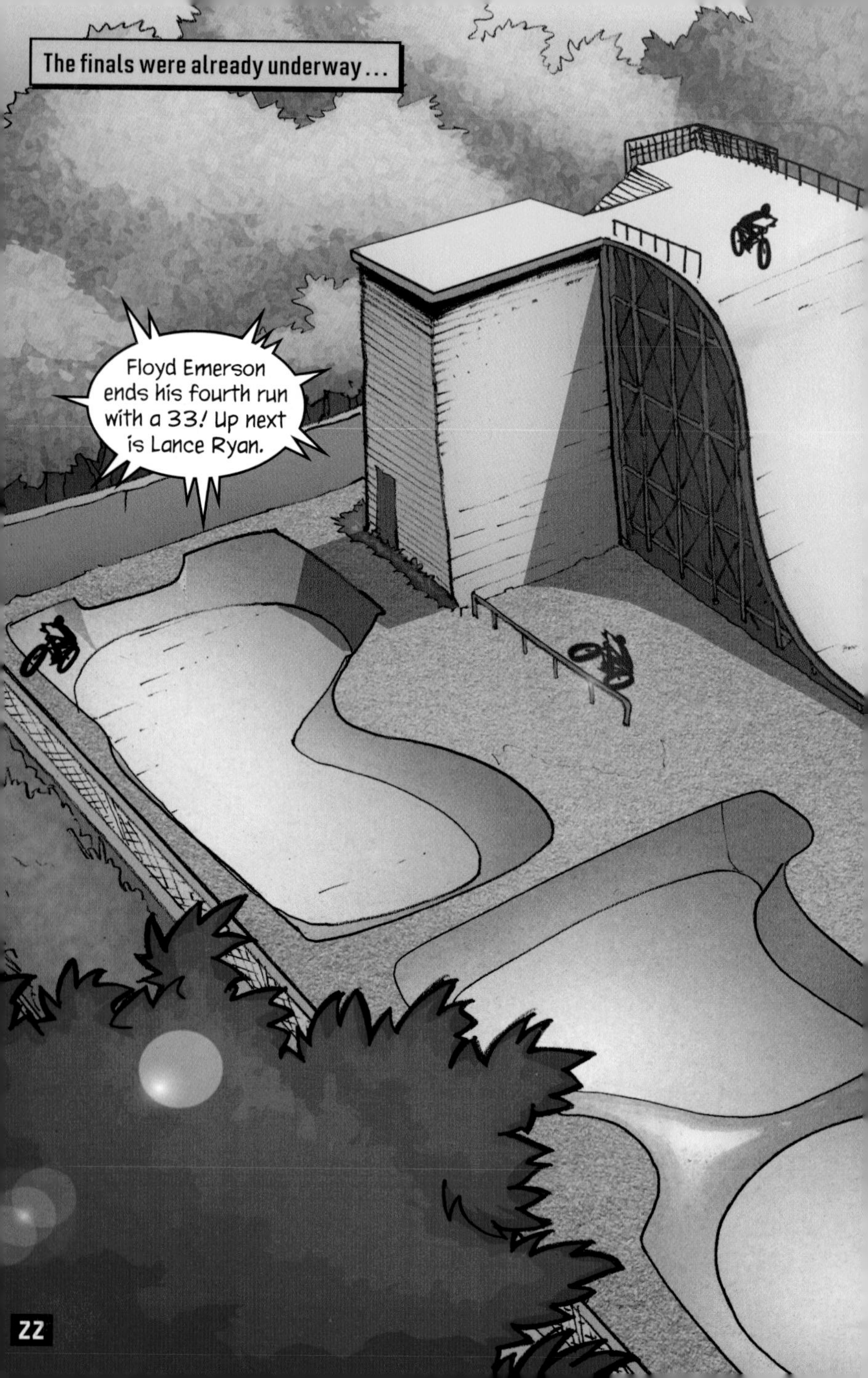
The finals were already underway . . .
Floyd Emerson ends his fourth run with a 33! Up next is Lance Ryan.

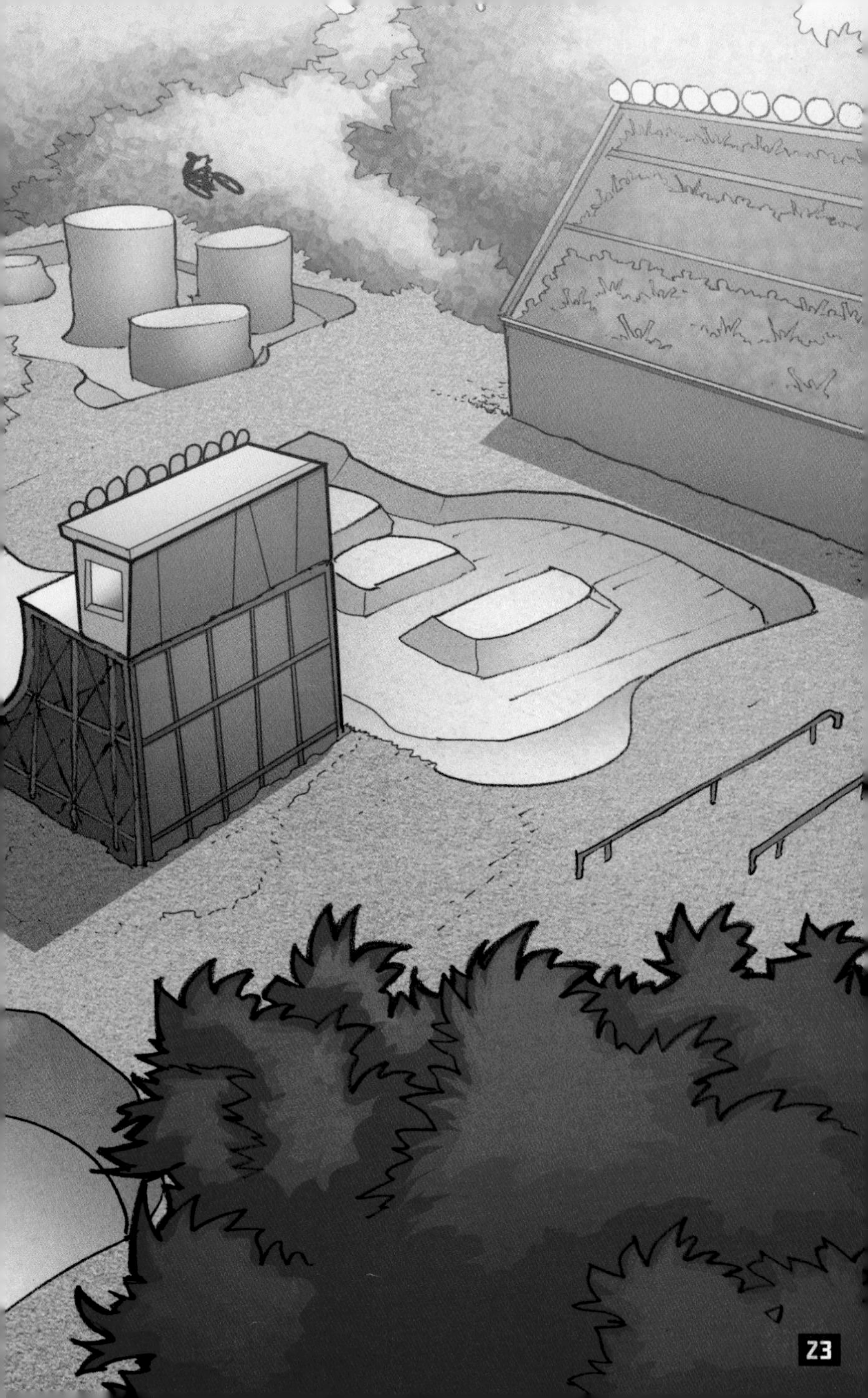

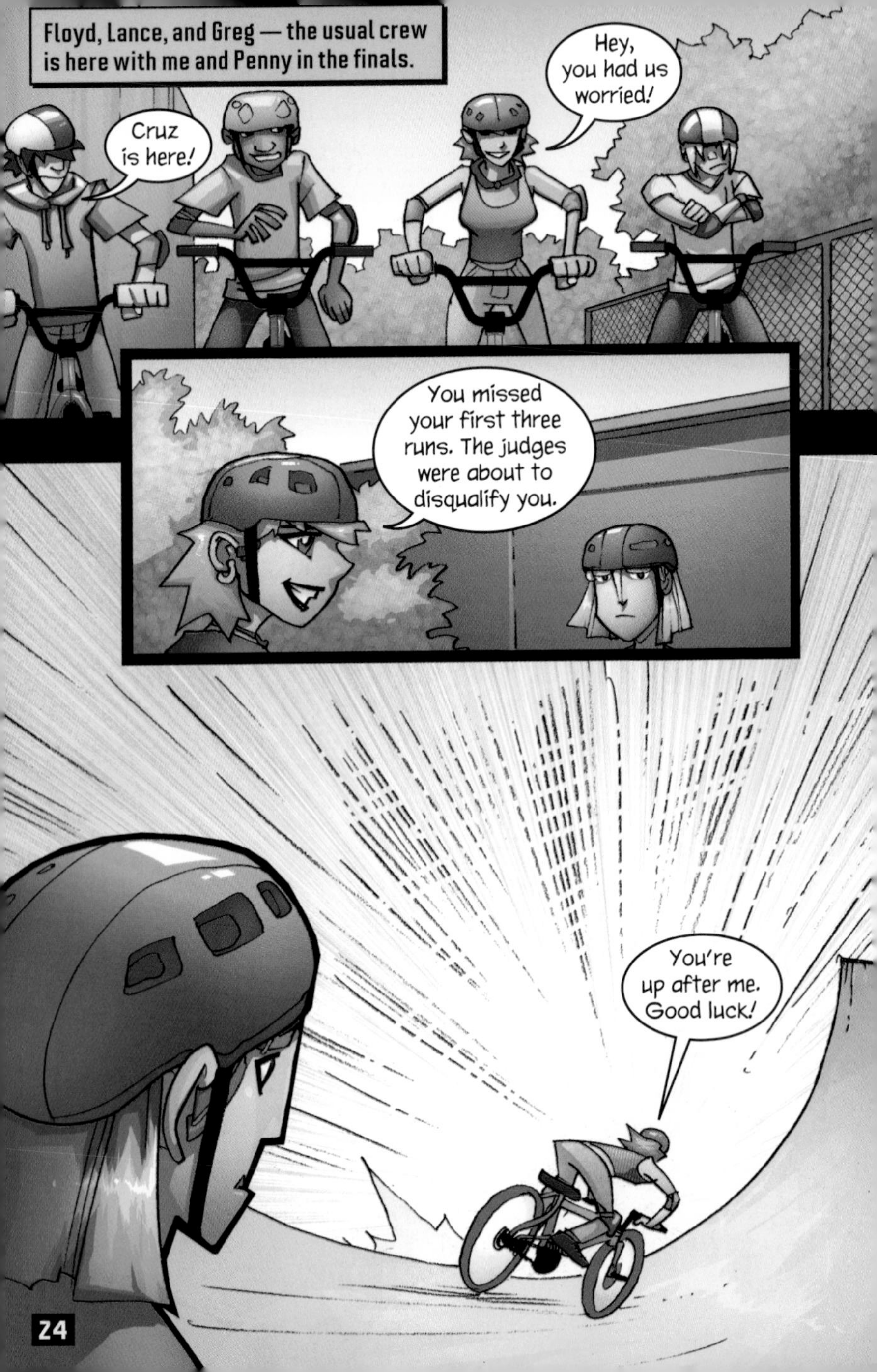
Floyd, Lance, and Greg — the usual crew is here with me and Penny in the finals.
Cruz is here!
Hey, you had us worried!
You missed your first three runs. The judges were about to disqualify you.
You're up after me. Good luck!

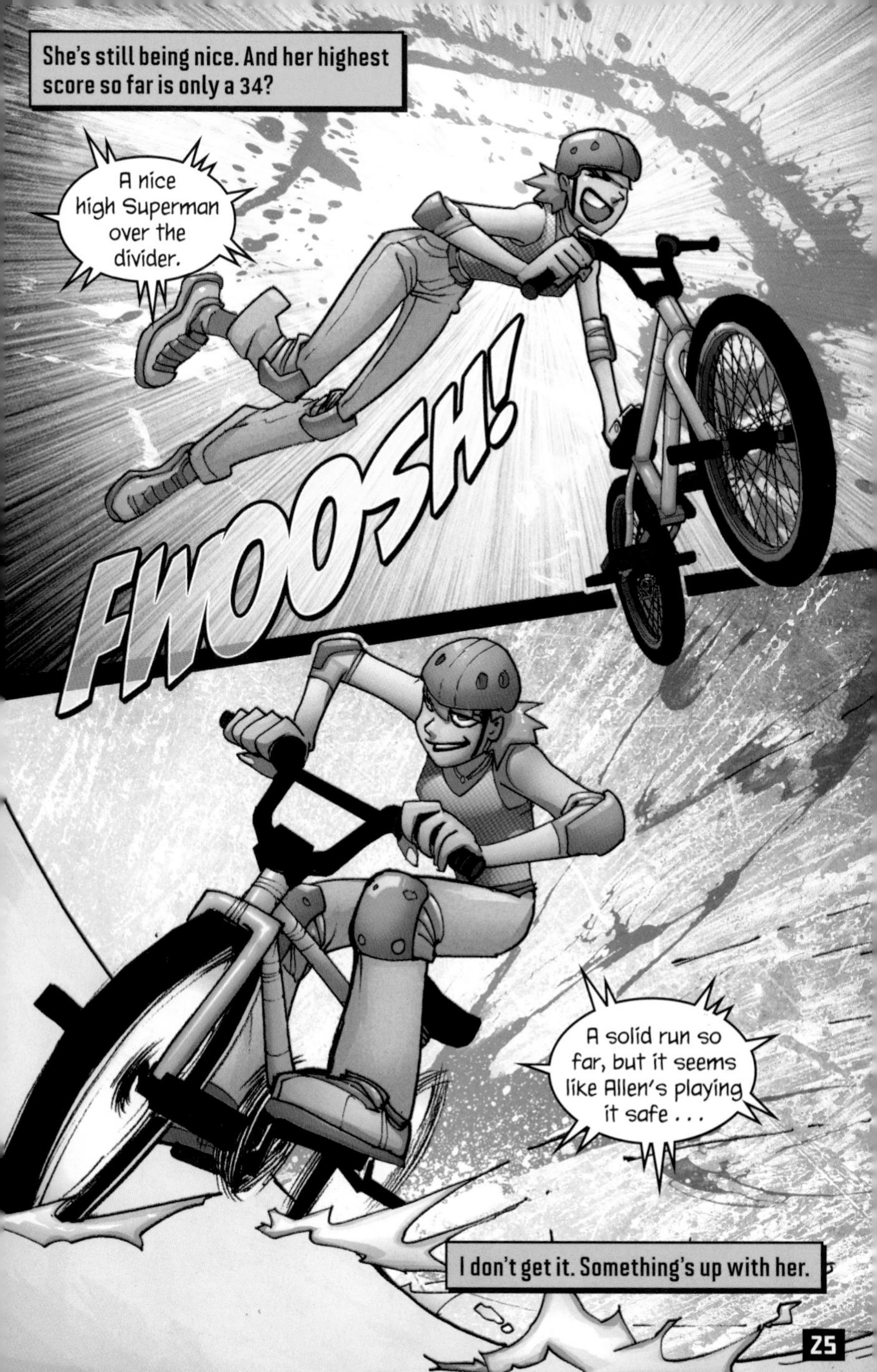
She's still being nice. And her highest score so far is only a 34?
A nice high Superman over the divider.
FWOOSH!
A solid run so far, but it seems like Allen's playing it safe . . .
I don't get it. Something's up with her.

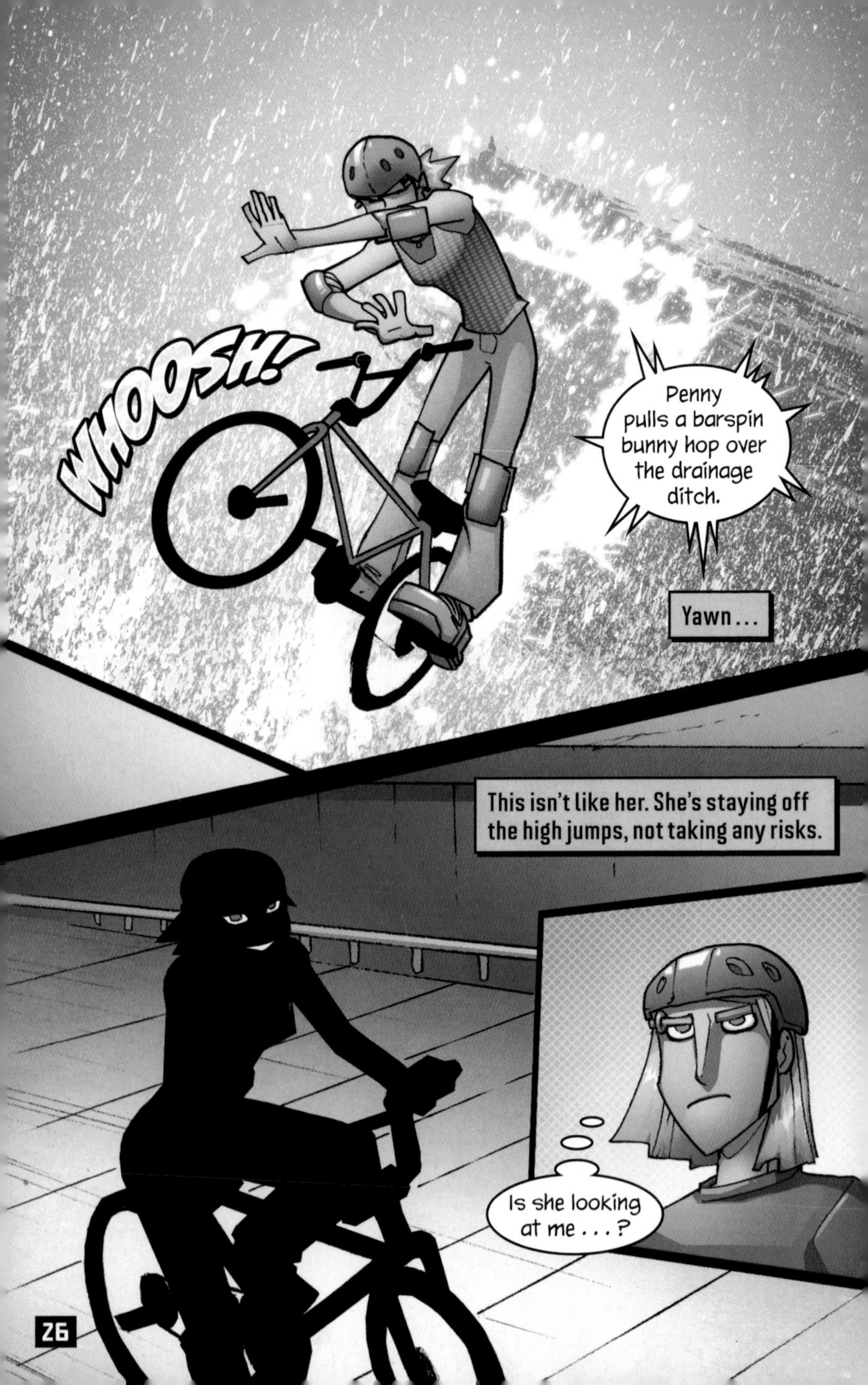
WHOOSH!
Penny pulls a barspin bunny hop over the drainage ditch.
Yawn . . .
This isn't like her. She's staying off the high jumps, not taking any risks.
Is she looking at me . . . ?

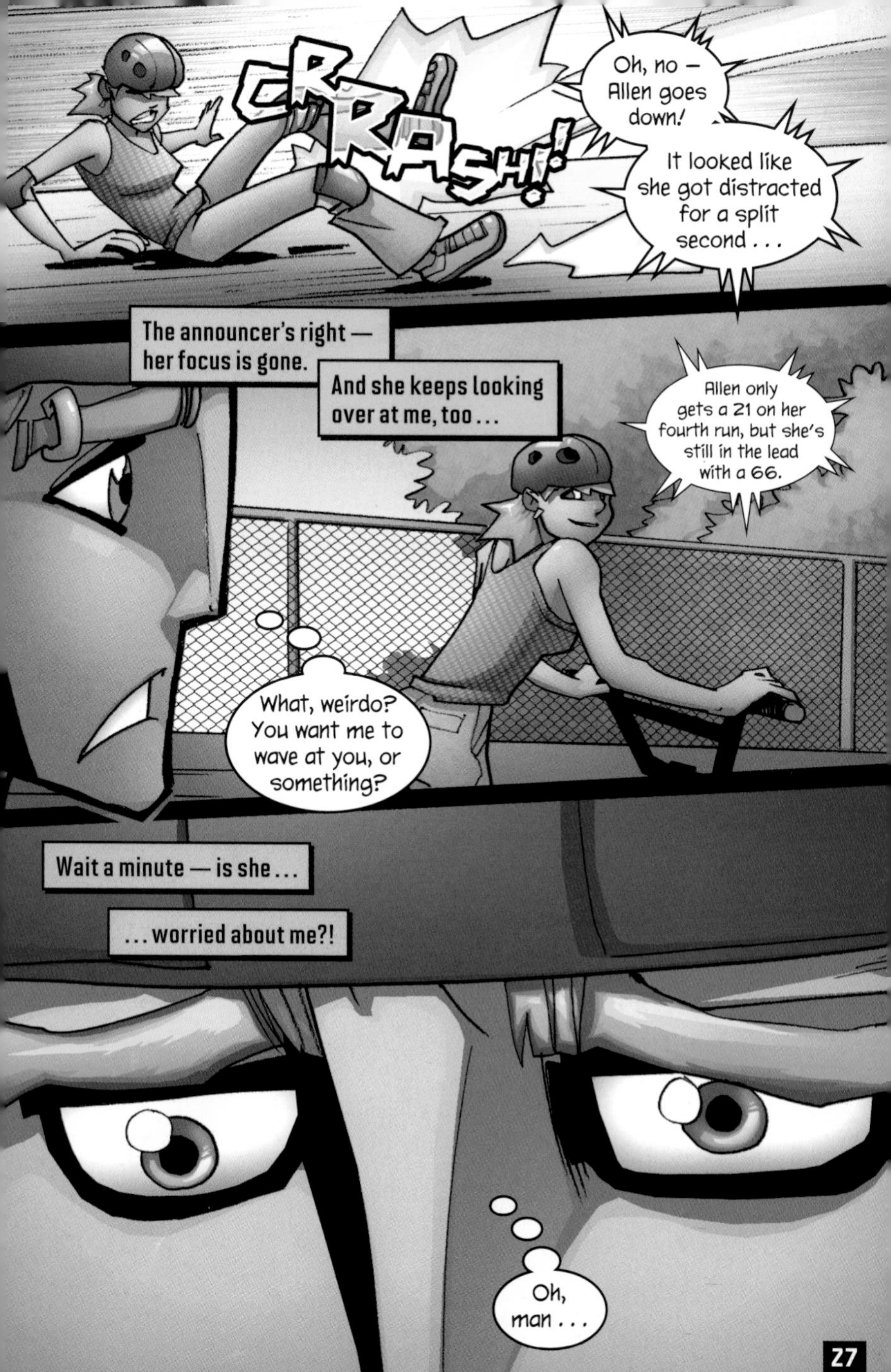
CRRASH!
Oh, no — Allen goes down!
It looked like she got distracted for a split second . . .
The announcer's right — her focus is gone.
And she keeps looking over at me, too . . .
Allen only gets a 21 on her fourth run, but she's still in the lead with a 66.
What, weirdo? You want me to wave at you, or something?
Wait a minute — is she . . .
. . . worried about me?!
Oh, man . . .

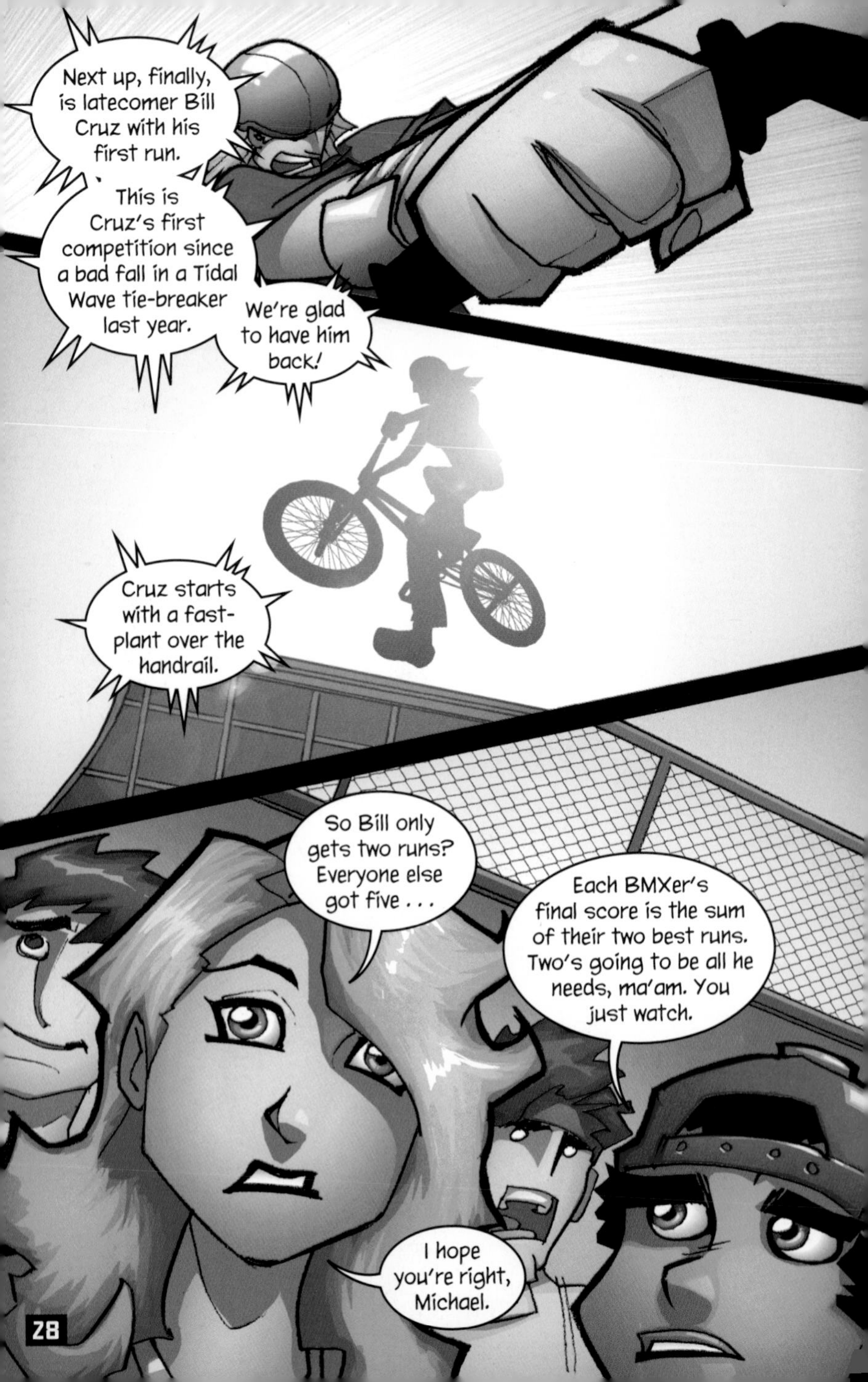
Next up, finally, is latecomer Bill Cruz with his first run.
This is Cruz's first competition since a bad fall in a Tidal Wave tie-breaker last year.
We're glad to have him back!
Cruz starts with a fast-plant over the handrail.
So Bill only gets two runs? Everyone else got five . . .
Each BMXer's final score is the sum of their two best runs. Two's going to be all he needs, ma'am. You just watch.
I hope you're right, Michael.

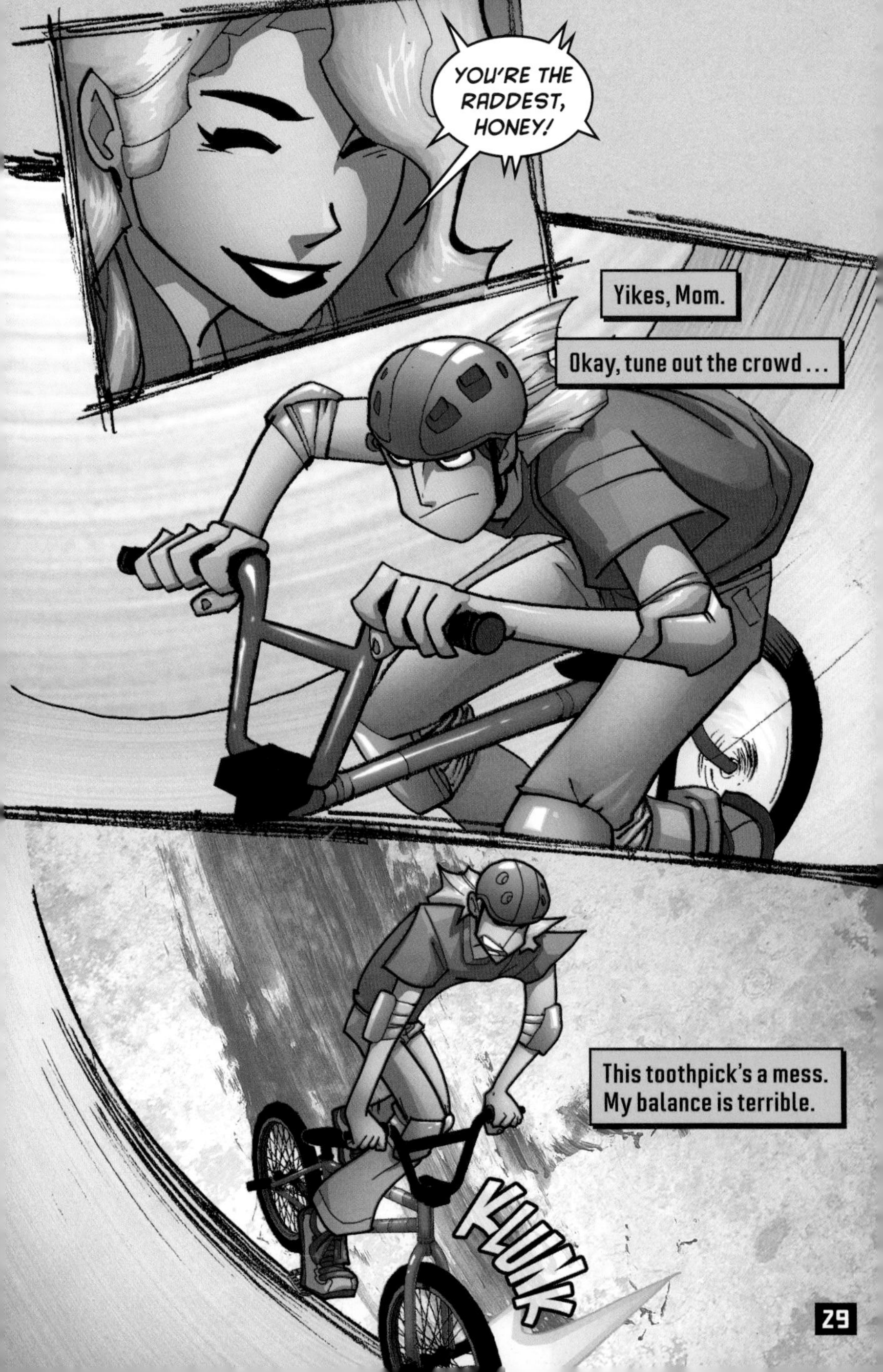
YOU'RE THE RADDEST, HONEY!
Yikes, Mom.
Okay, tune out the crowd . . .
This toothpick's a mess. My balance is terrible.
KLUNK

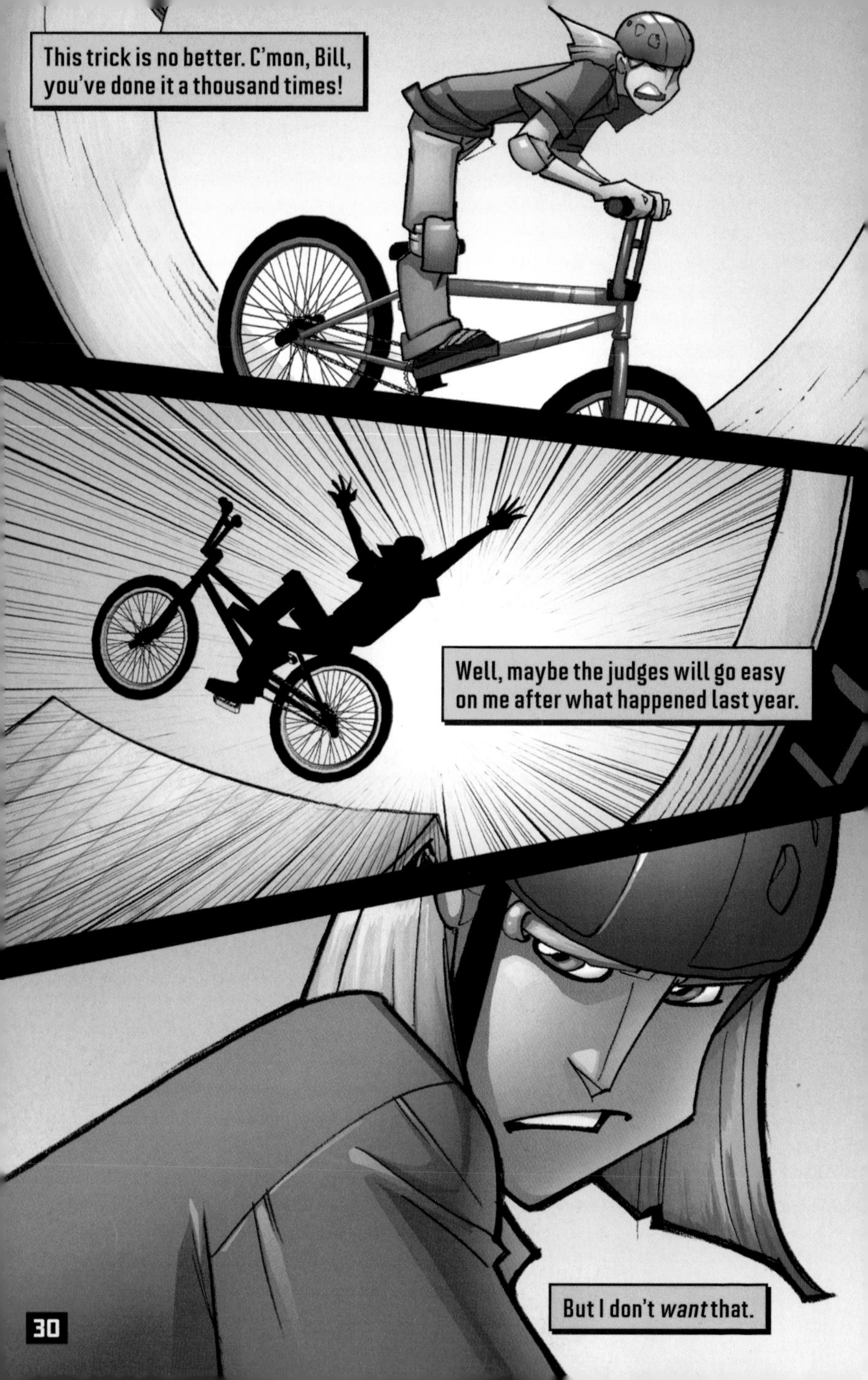
This trick is no better. C'mon, Bill, you've done it a thousand times!
Well, maybe the judges will go easy on me after what happened last year.
But I don't *want* that.

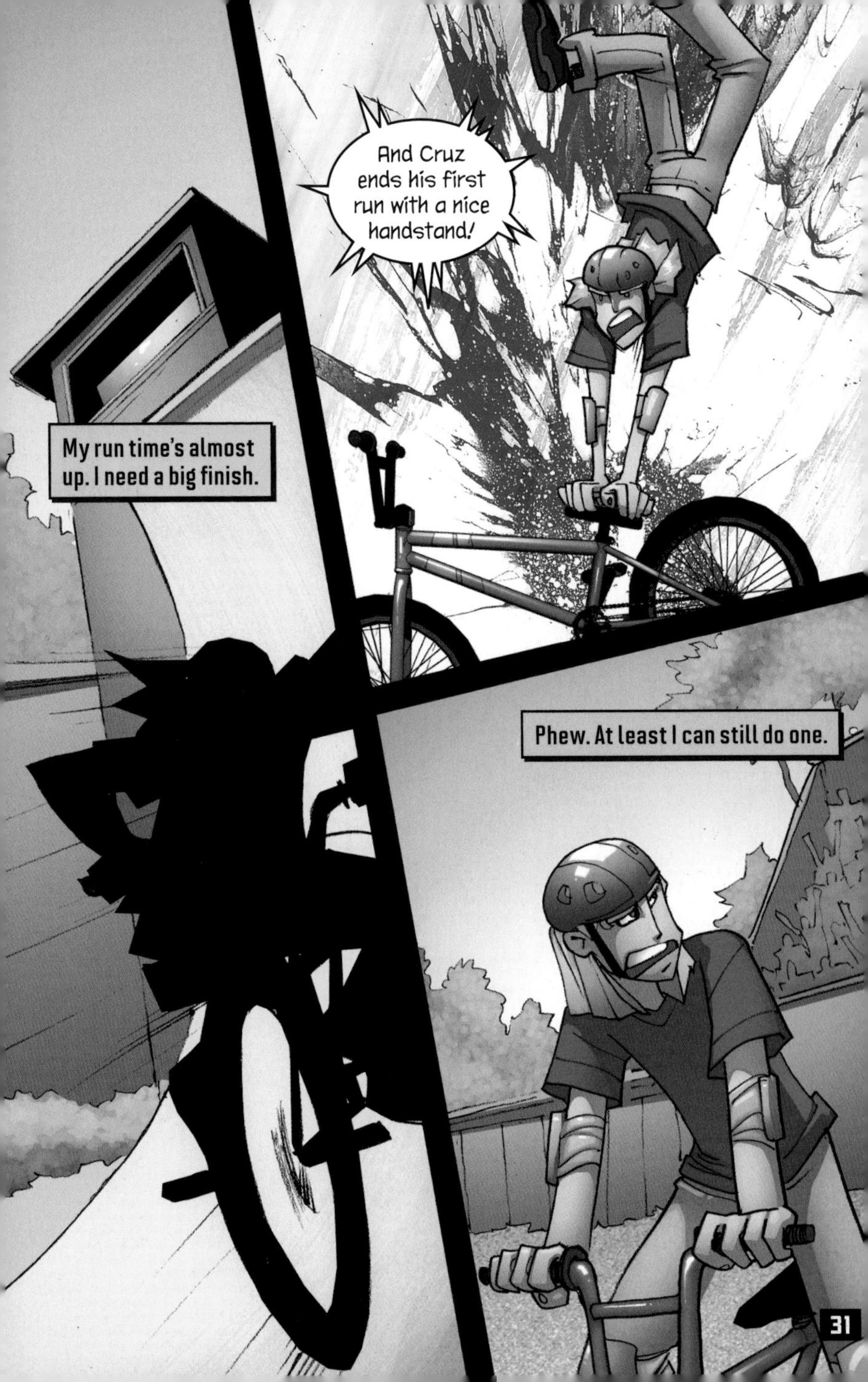
My run time's almost up. I need a big finish.
And Cruz ends his first run with a nice handstand!
Phew. At least I can still do one.

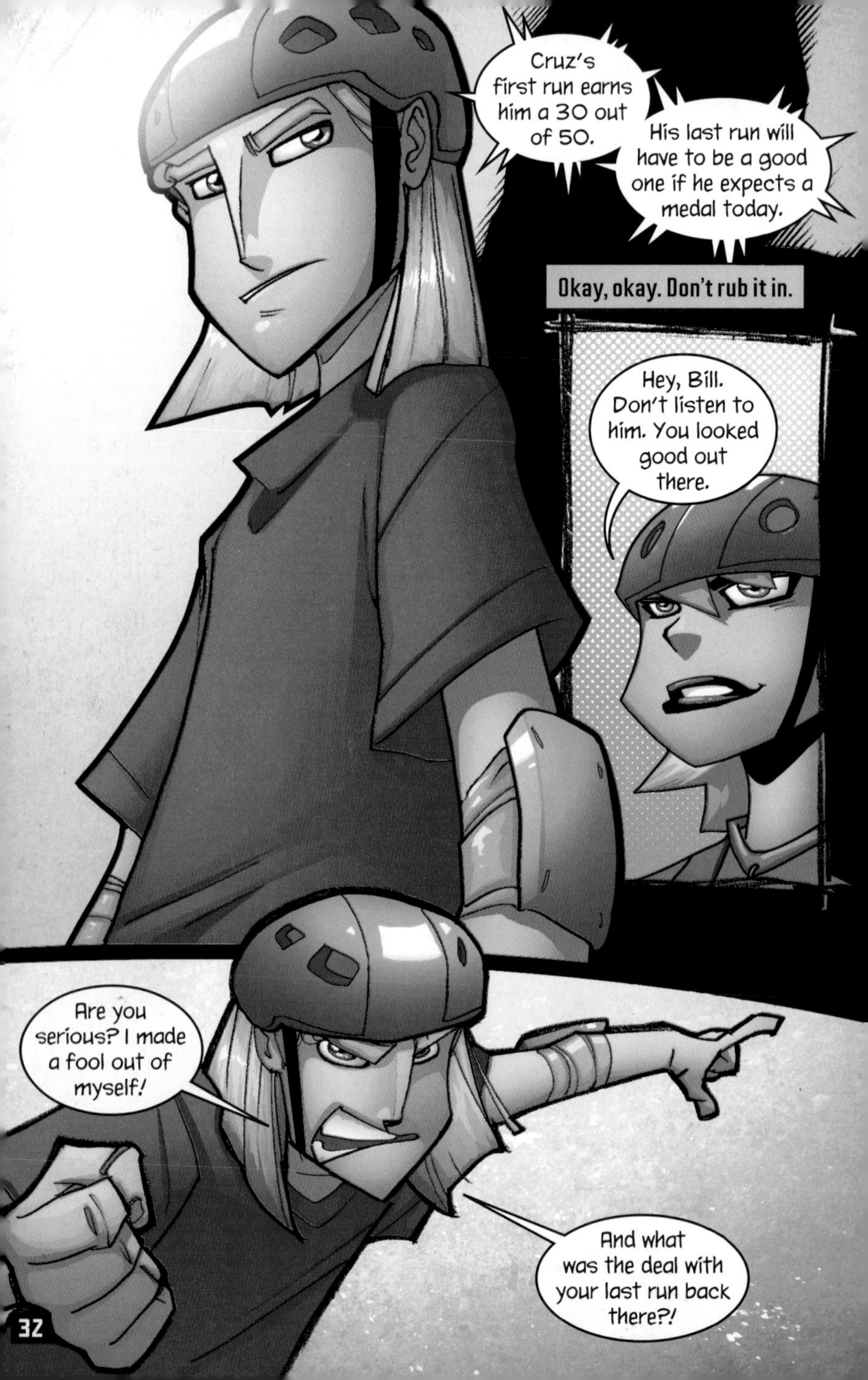
Cruz's first run earns him a 30 out of 50.
His last run will have to be a good one if he expects a medal today.
Okay, okay. Don't rub it in.
Hey, Bill. Don't listen to him. You looked good out there.
Are you serious? I made a fool out of myself!
And what was the deal with your last run back there?!

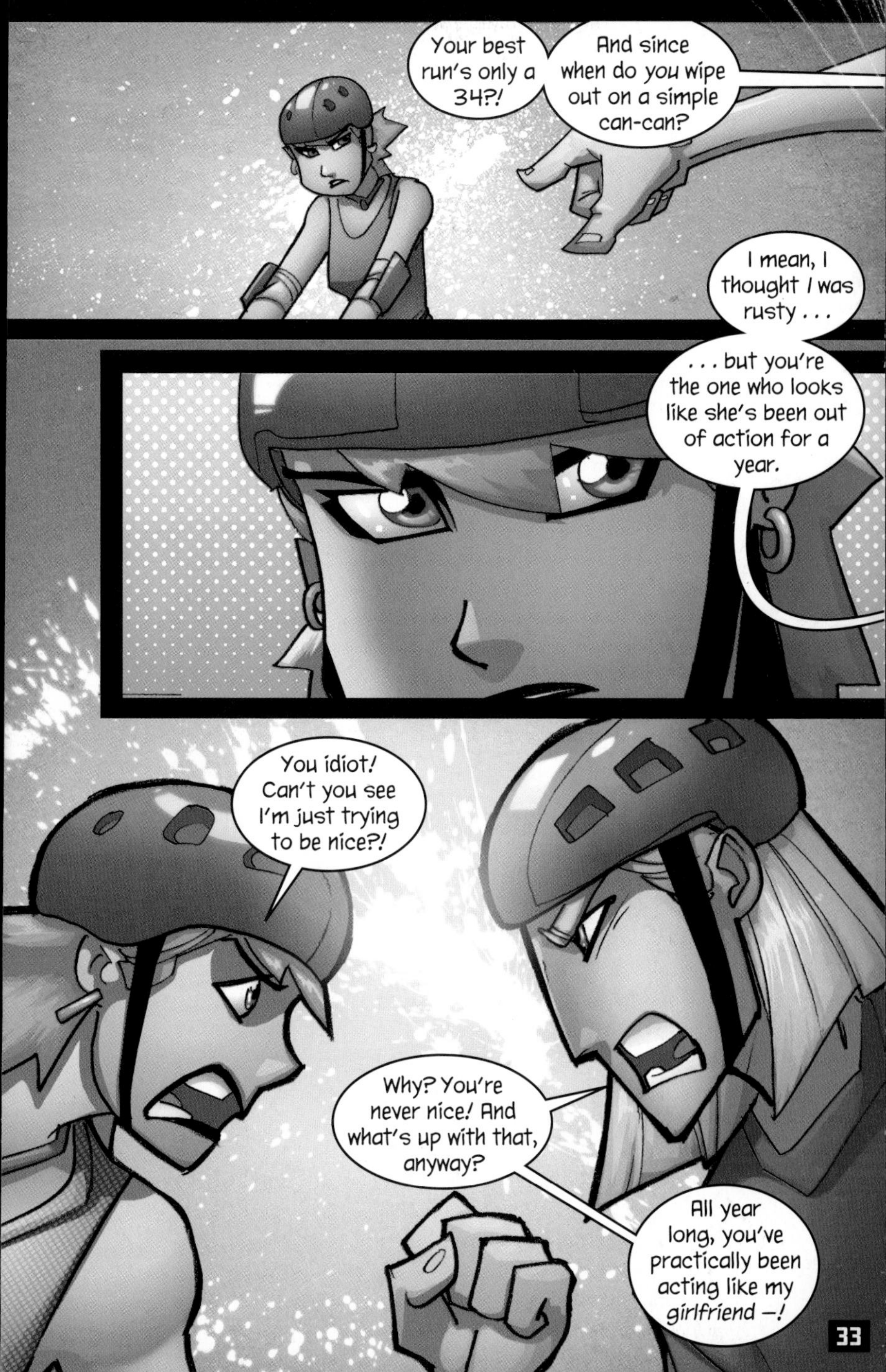
Your best run's only a 34?!
And since when do you wipe out on a simple can-can?
I mean, I thought I was rusty . . .
. . . but you're the one who looks like she's been out of action for a year.
You idiot! Can't you see I'm just trying to be nice?!
Why? You're never nice! And what's up with that, anyway?
All year long, you've practically been acting like my girlfriend —!

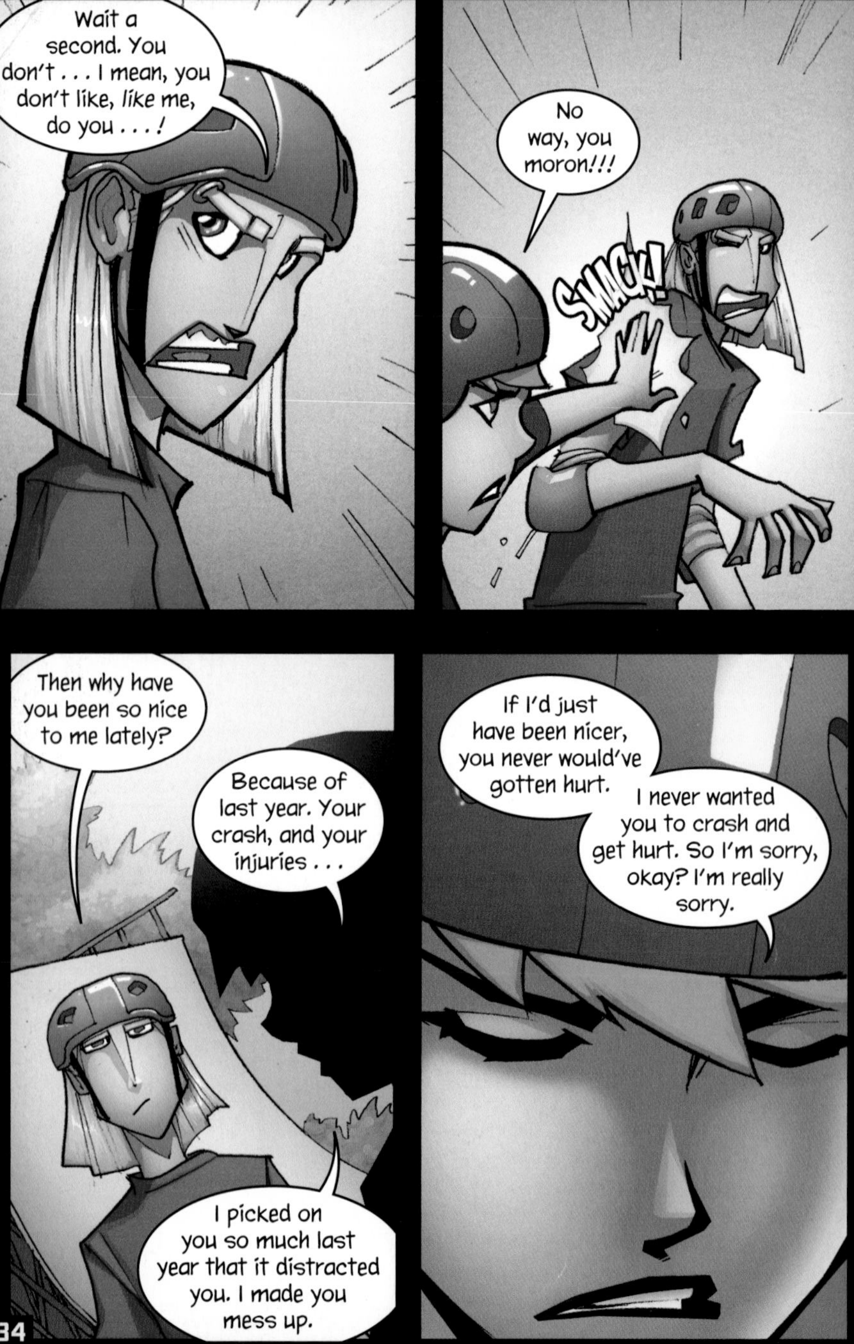
Wait a second. You don't . . . I mean, you don't like, *like* me, do you . . . !
No way, you moron!!!
SMACK!
Then why have you been so nice to me lately?
Because of last year. Your crash, and your injuries . . .
I picked on you so much last year that it distracted you. I made you mess up.
If I'd just have been nicer, you never would've gotten hurt.
I never wanted you to crash and get hurt. So I'm sorry, okay? I'm really sorry.

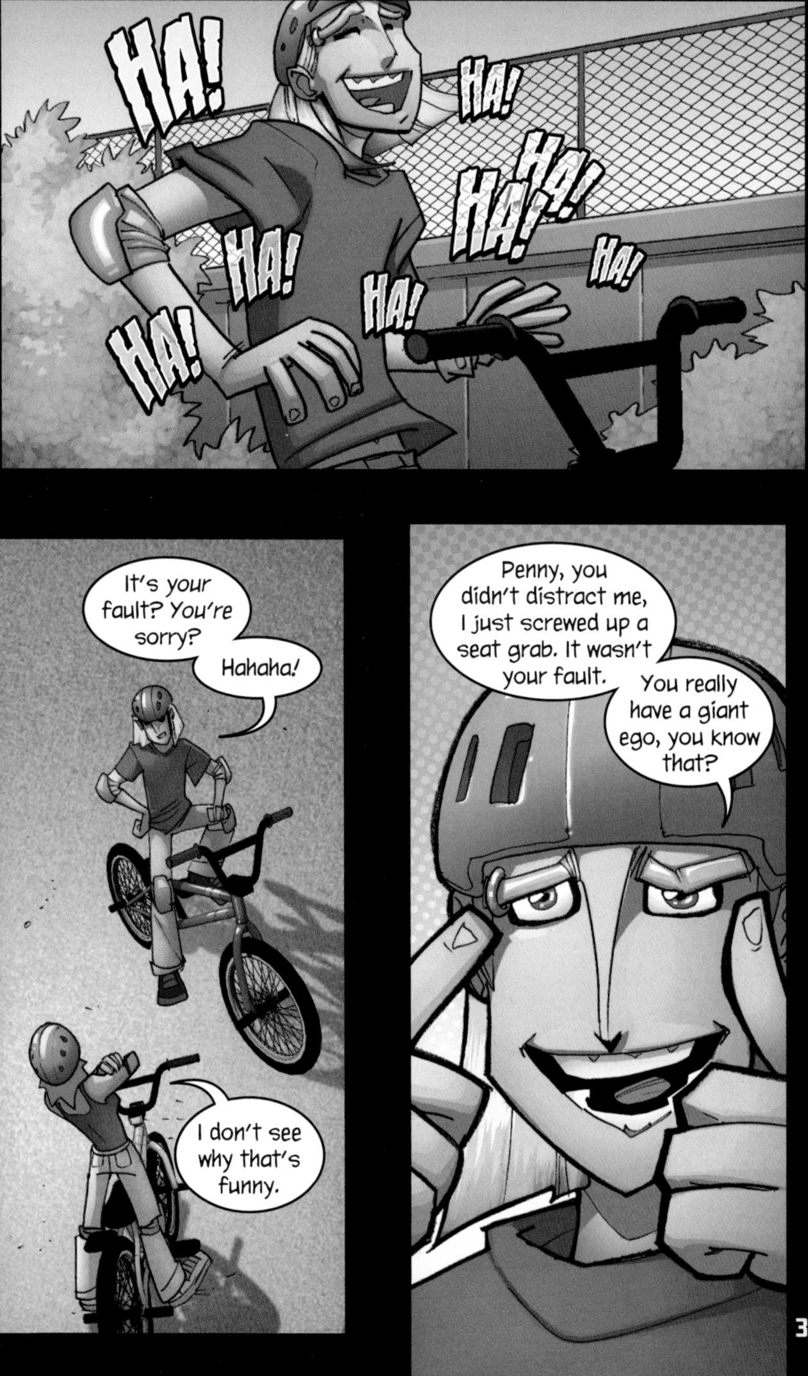
HA!
HA!
HA!
HA!
HA!
HA!
HA!
HA!
It's your fault? You're sorry?
Hahaha!
I don't see why that's funny.
Penny, you didn't distract me, I just screwed up a seat grab. It wasn't your fault.
You really have a giant ego, you know that?

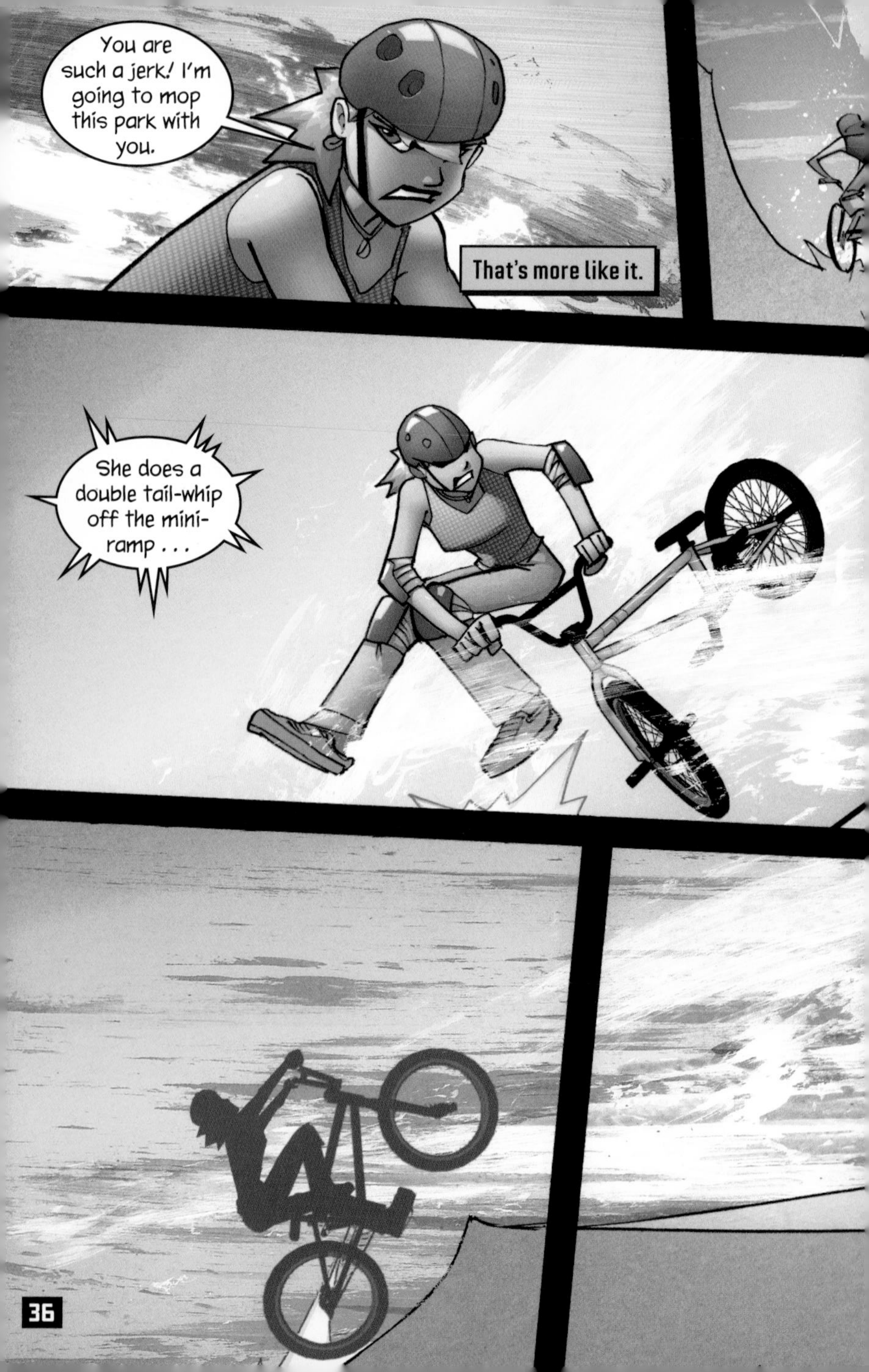
You are such a jerk! I'm going to mop this park with you.
That's more like it.
She does a double tail-whip off the mini-ramp . . .

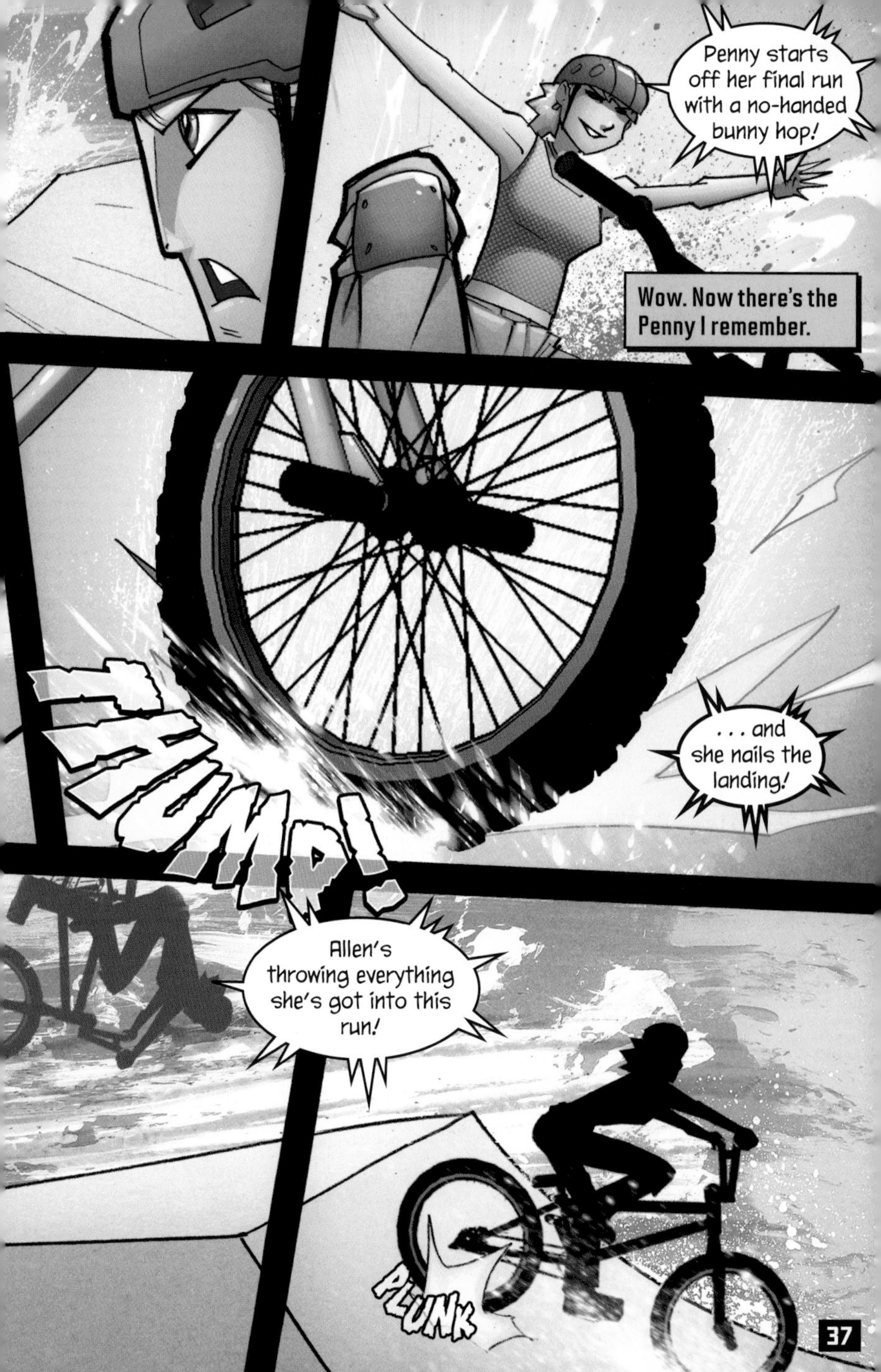
Penny starts off her final run with a no-handed bunny hop!
Wow. Now there's the Penny I remember.
THUMP!
. . . and she nails the landing!
Allen's throwing everything she's got into this run!
PLUNK

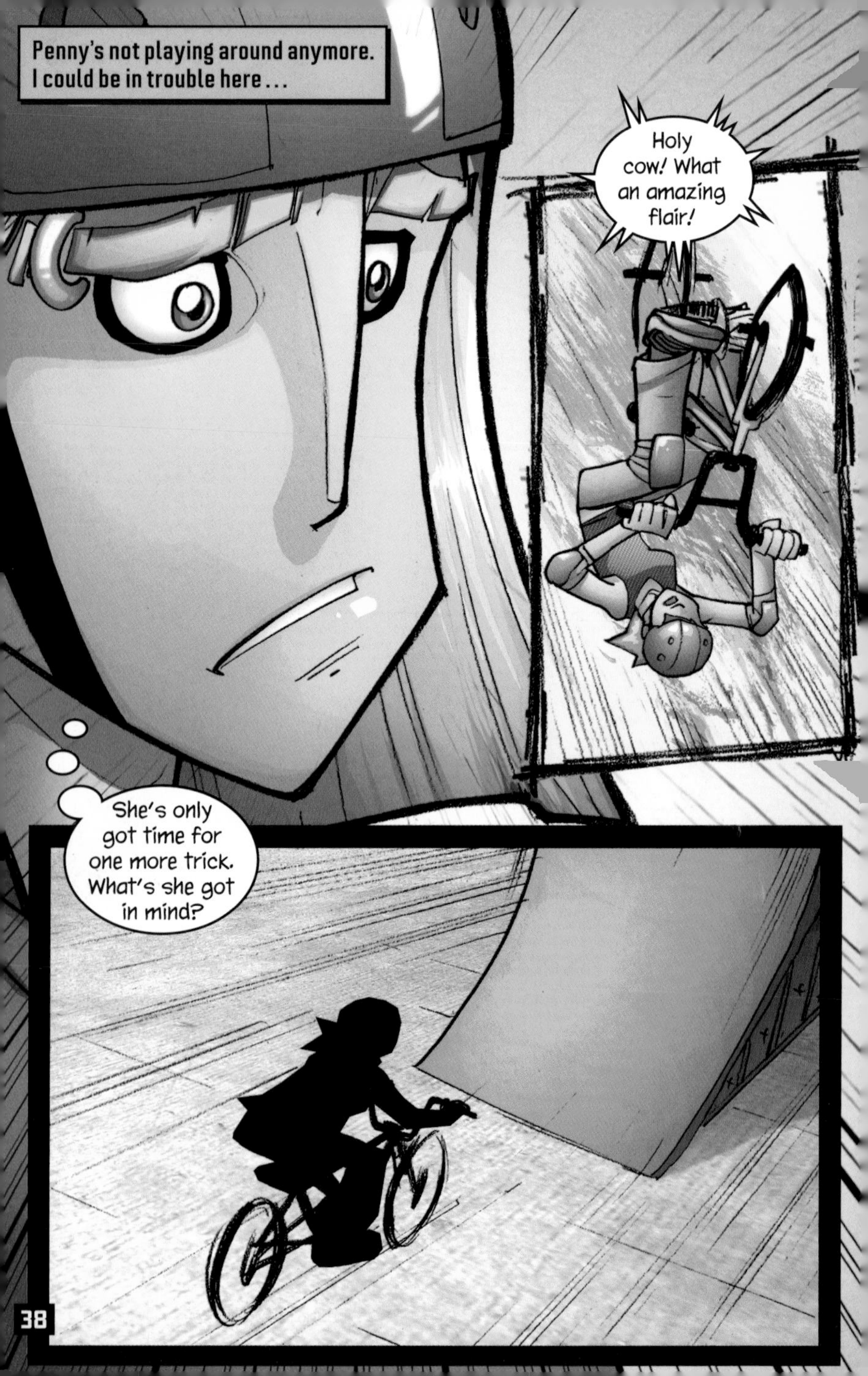
Penny's not playing around anymore. I could be in trouble here . . .
Holy cow! What an amazing flair!
She's only got time for one more trick. What's she got in mind?

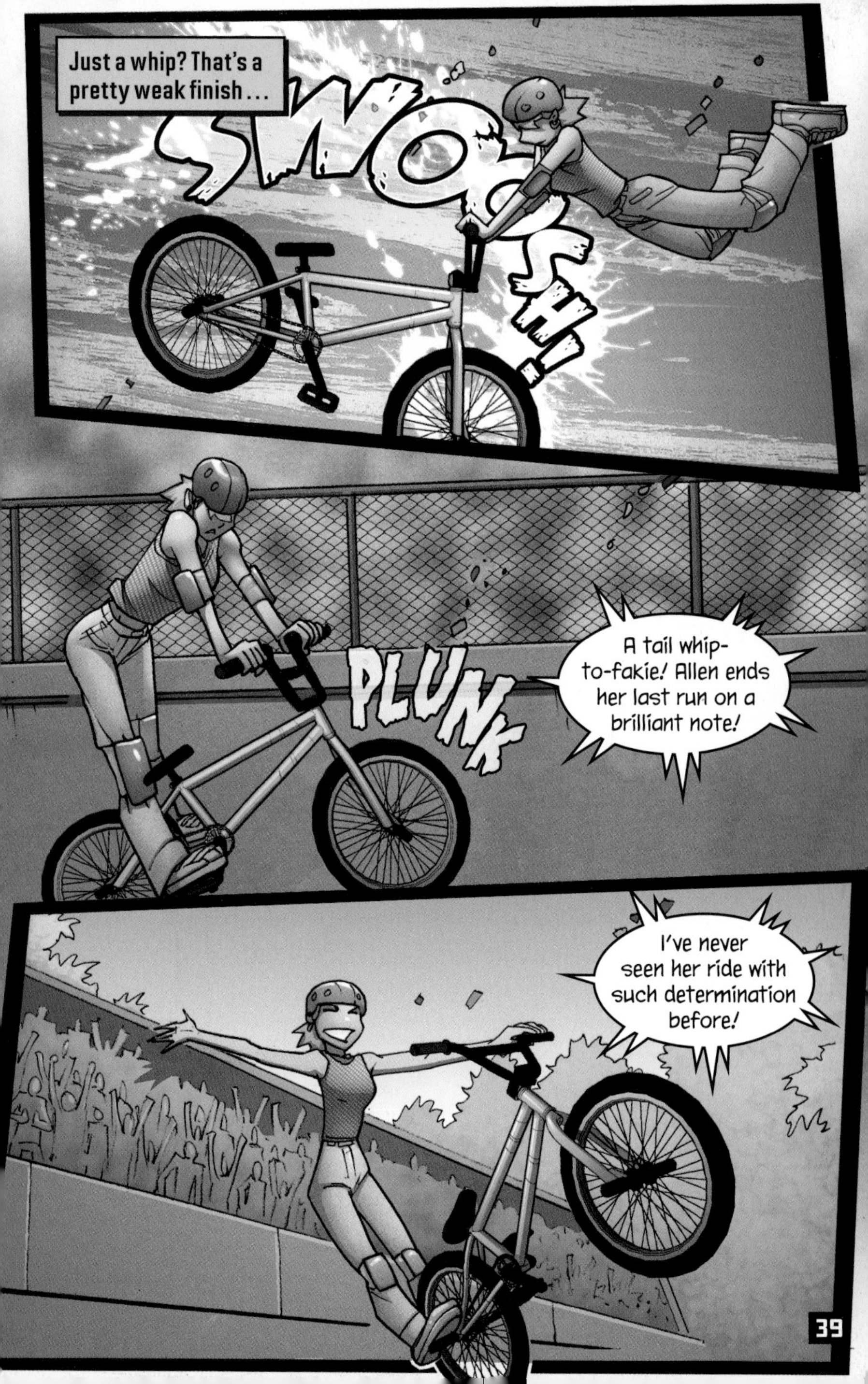
Just a whip? That's a pretty weak finish . . .
SWOOSH!
PLUNK
A tail whip-to-fakie! Allen ends her last run on a brilliant note!
I've never seen her ride with such determination before!

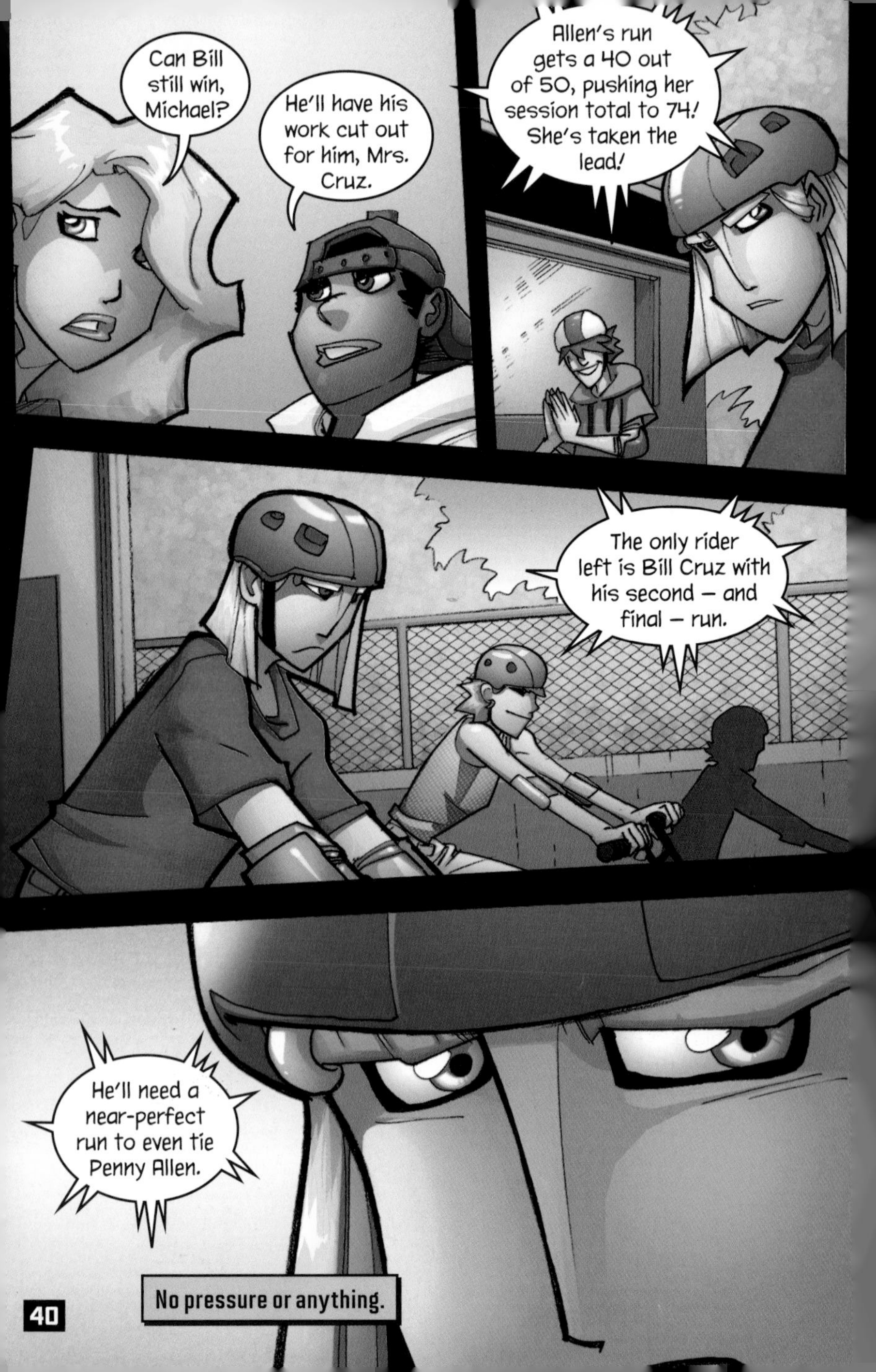

Can Bill still win, Michael?
He'll have his work cut out for him, Mrs. Cruz.
Allen's run gets a 40 out of 50, pushing her session total to 74! She's taken the lead!
The only rider left is Bill Cruz with his second — and final — run.
He'll need a near-perfect run to even tie Penny Allen.
No pressure or anything.

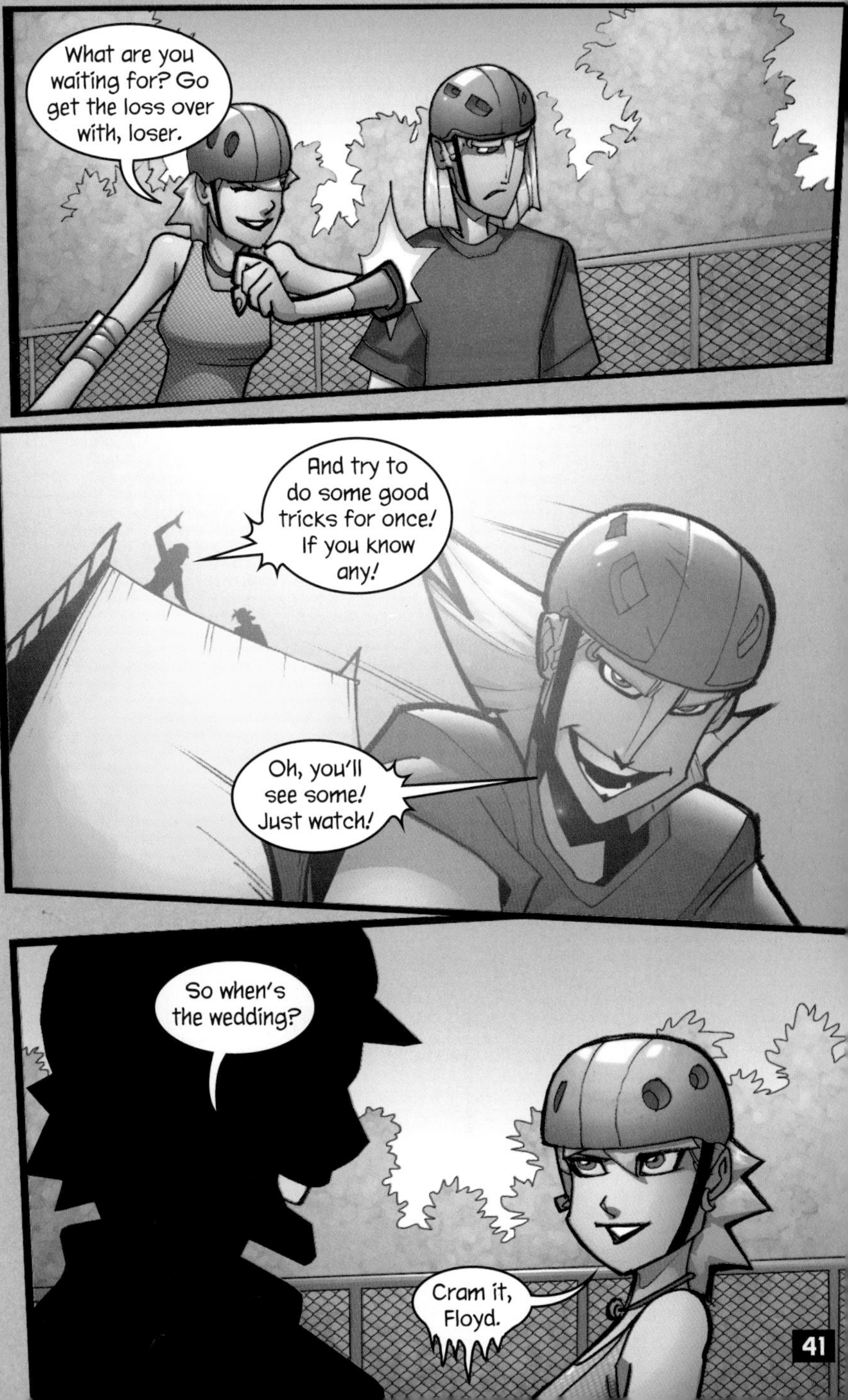
What are you waiting for? Go get the loss over with, loser.
And try to do some good tricks for once! If you know any!
Oh, you'll see some! Just watch!
So when's the wedding?
Cram it, Floyd.

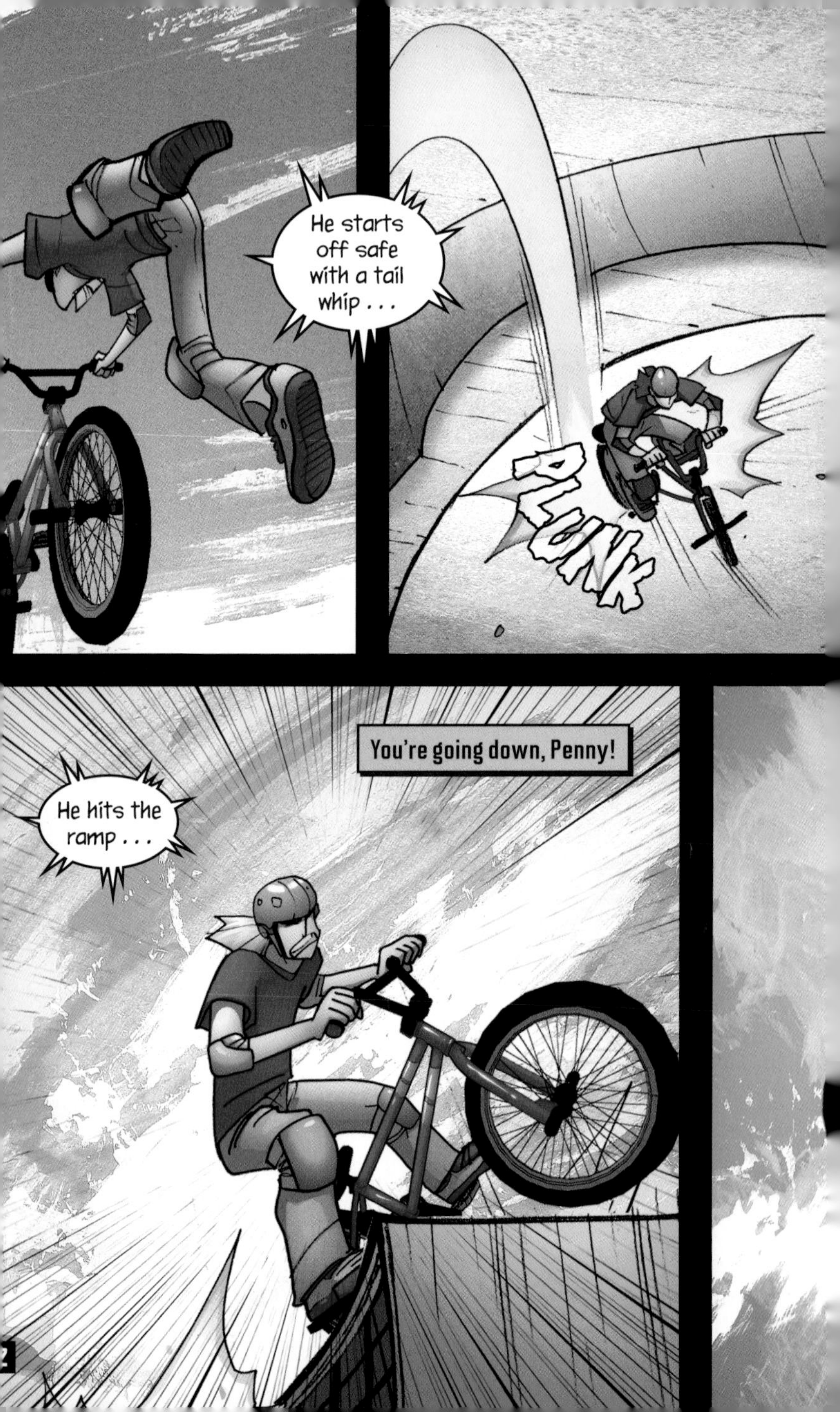
He starts off safe with a tail whip . . .
PLUNK
He hits the ramp . . .
You're going down, Penny!

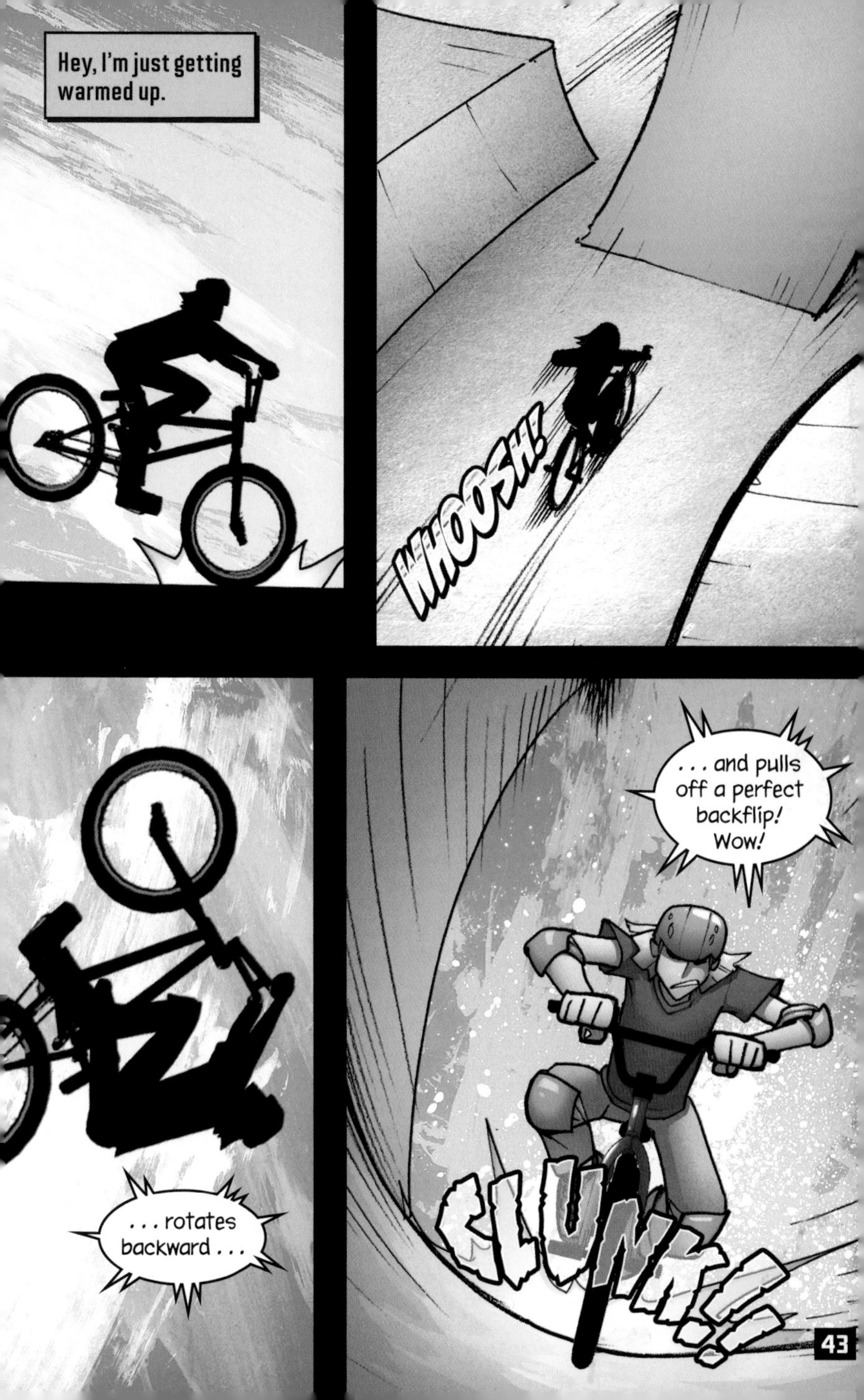
Hey, I'm just getting warmed up.
WHOOSH!
. . . rotates backward . . .
. . . and pulls off a perfect backflip! Wow!
CLUNK!!

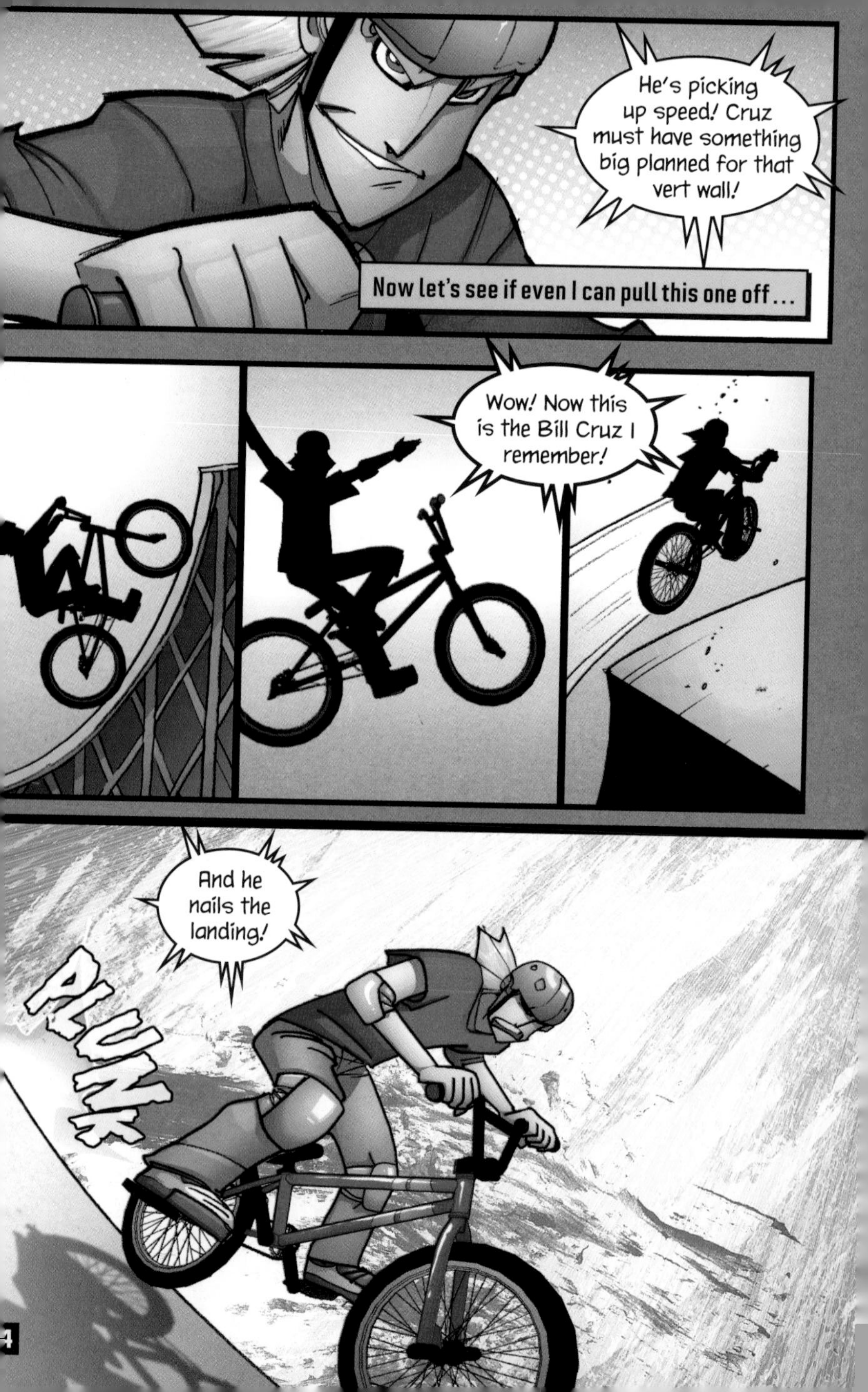
He's picking up speed! Cruz must have something big planned for that vert wall!
Now let's see if even I can pull this one off...
Wow! Now this is the Bill Cruz I remember!
And he nails the landing!
PLUNK

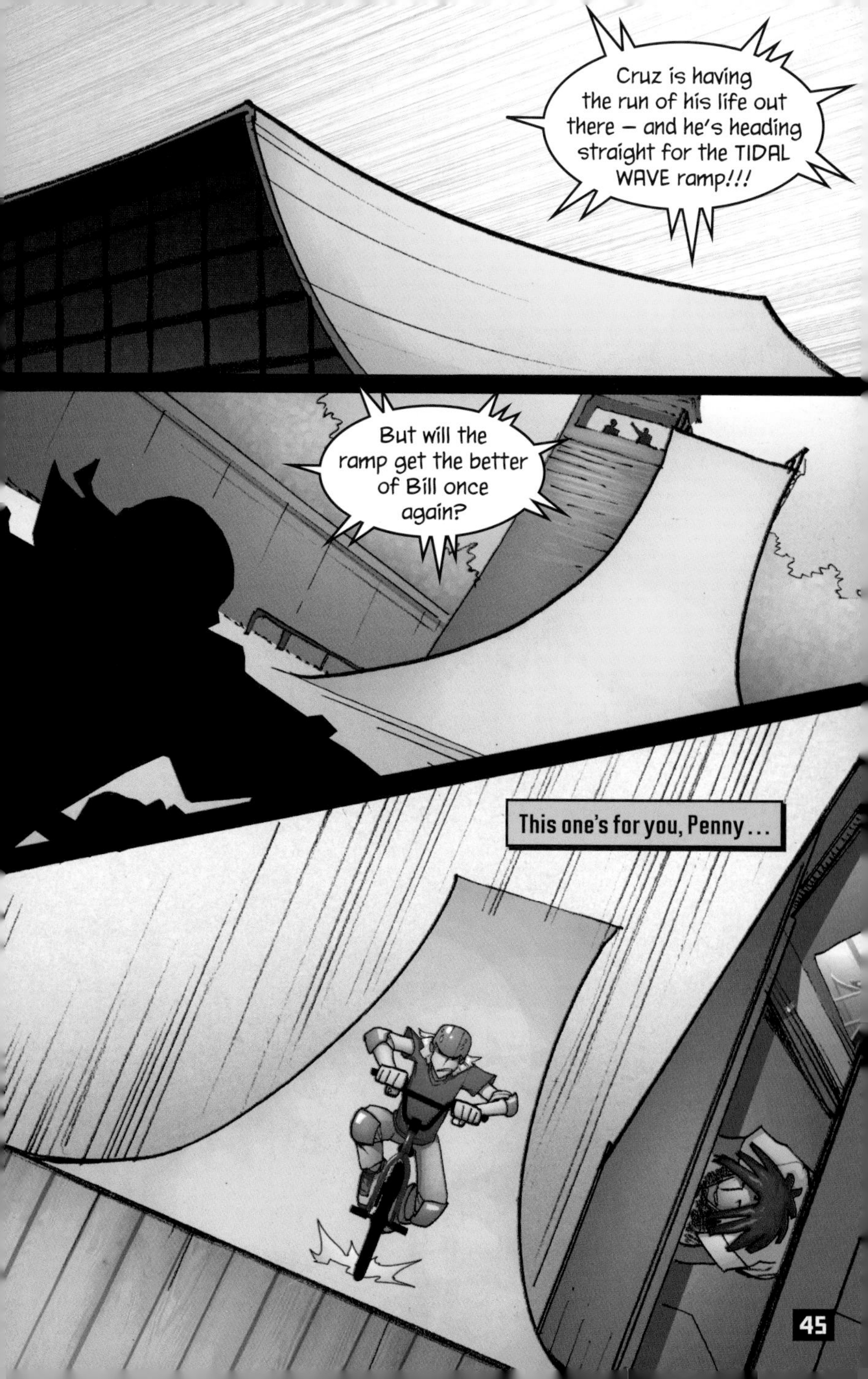
Cruz is having the run of his life out there — and he's heading straight for the TIDAL WAVE ramp!!!
But will the ramp get the better of Bill once again?
This one's for you, Penny . . .

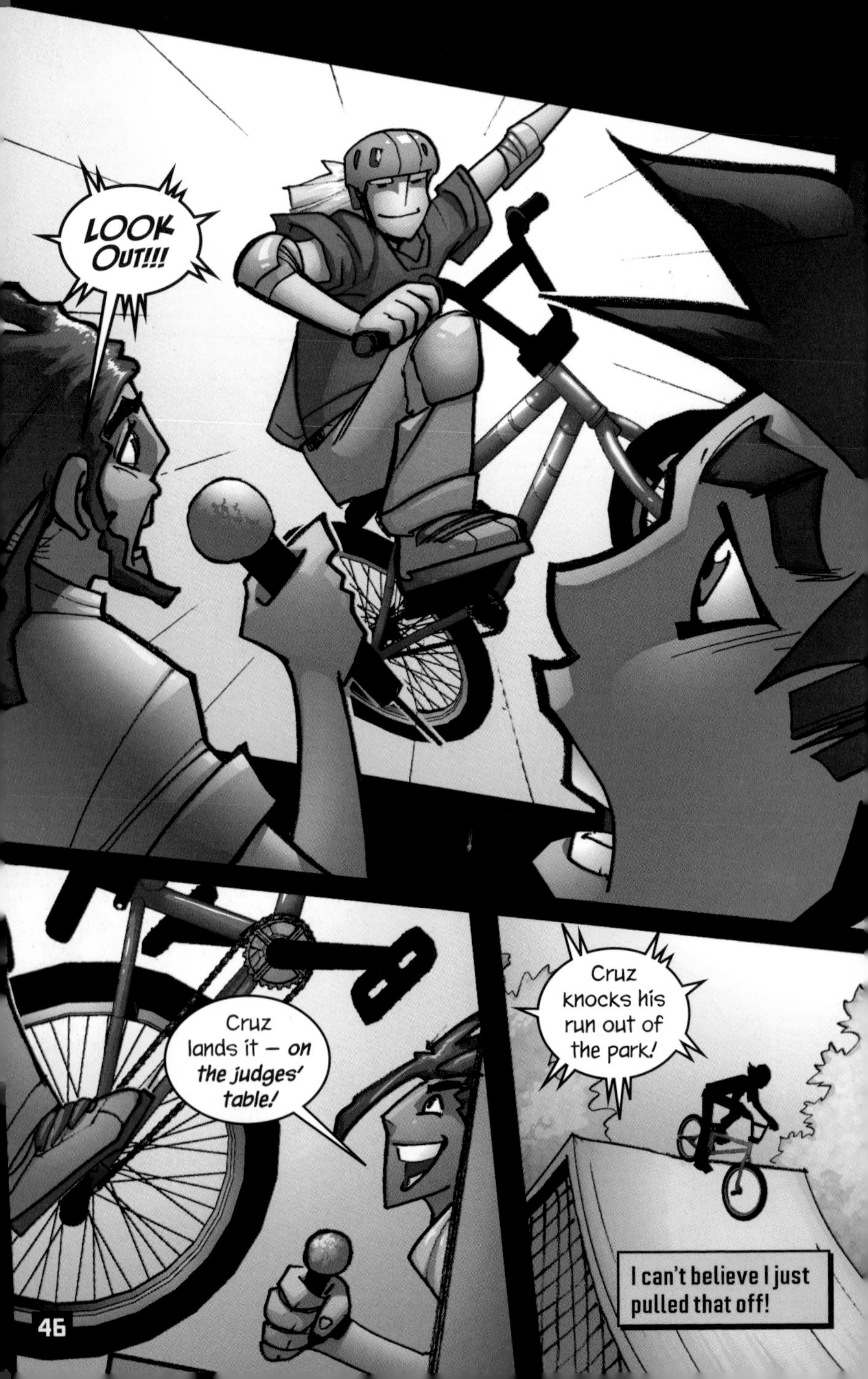
LOOK OUT!!!
Cruz lands it — *on the judges' table!*
Cruz knocks his run out of the park!
I can't believe I just pulled that off!

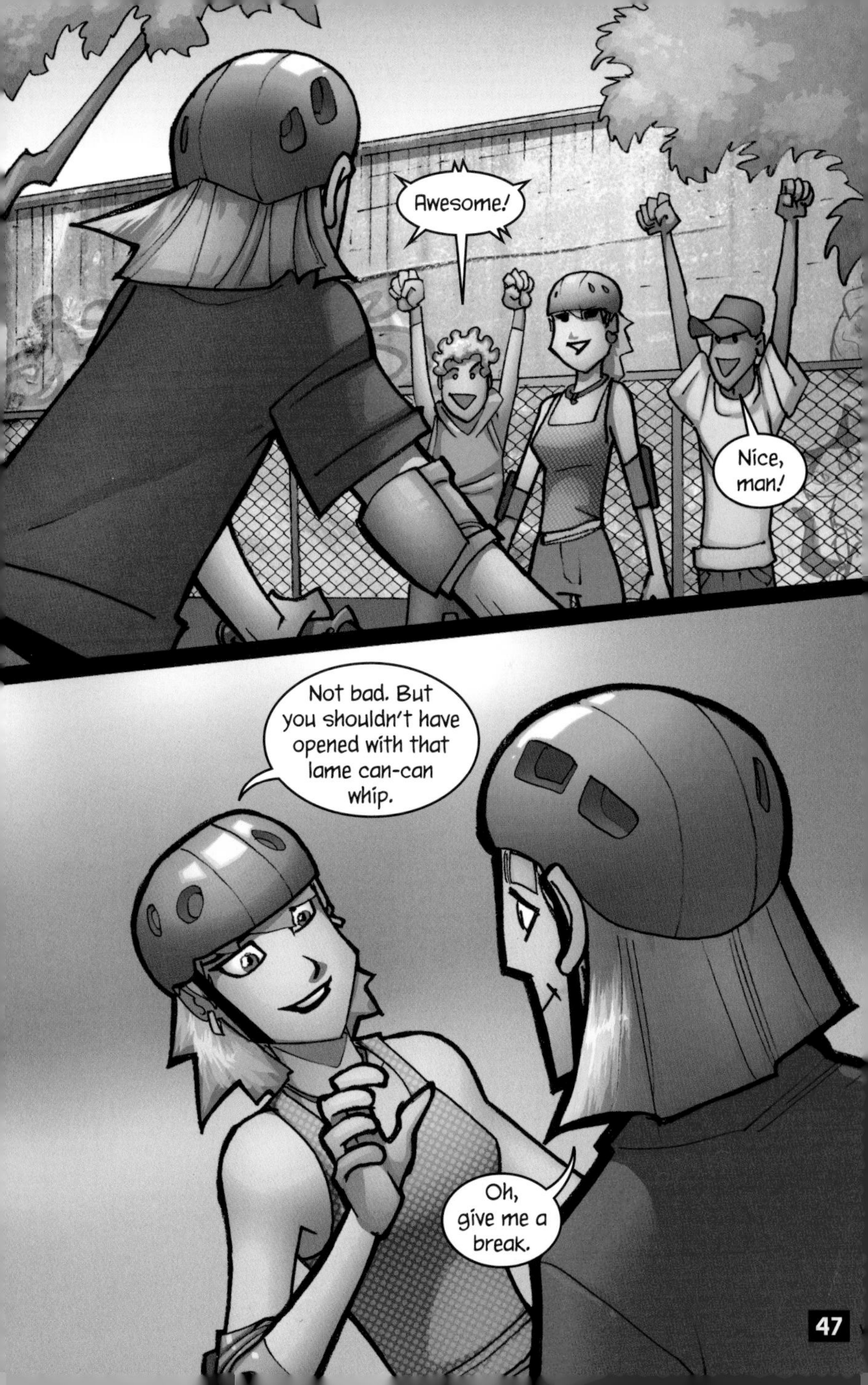
Awesome!
Nice, man!
Not bad. But you shouldn't have opened with that lame can-can whip.
Oh, give me a break.

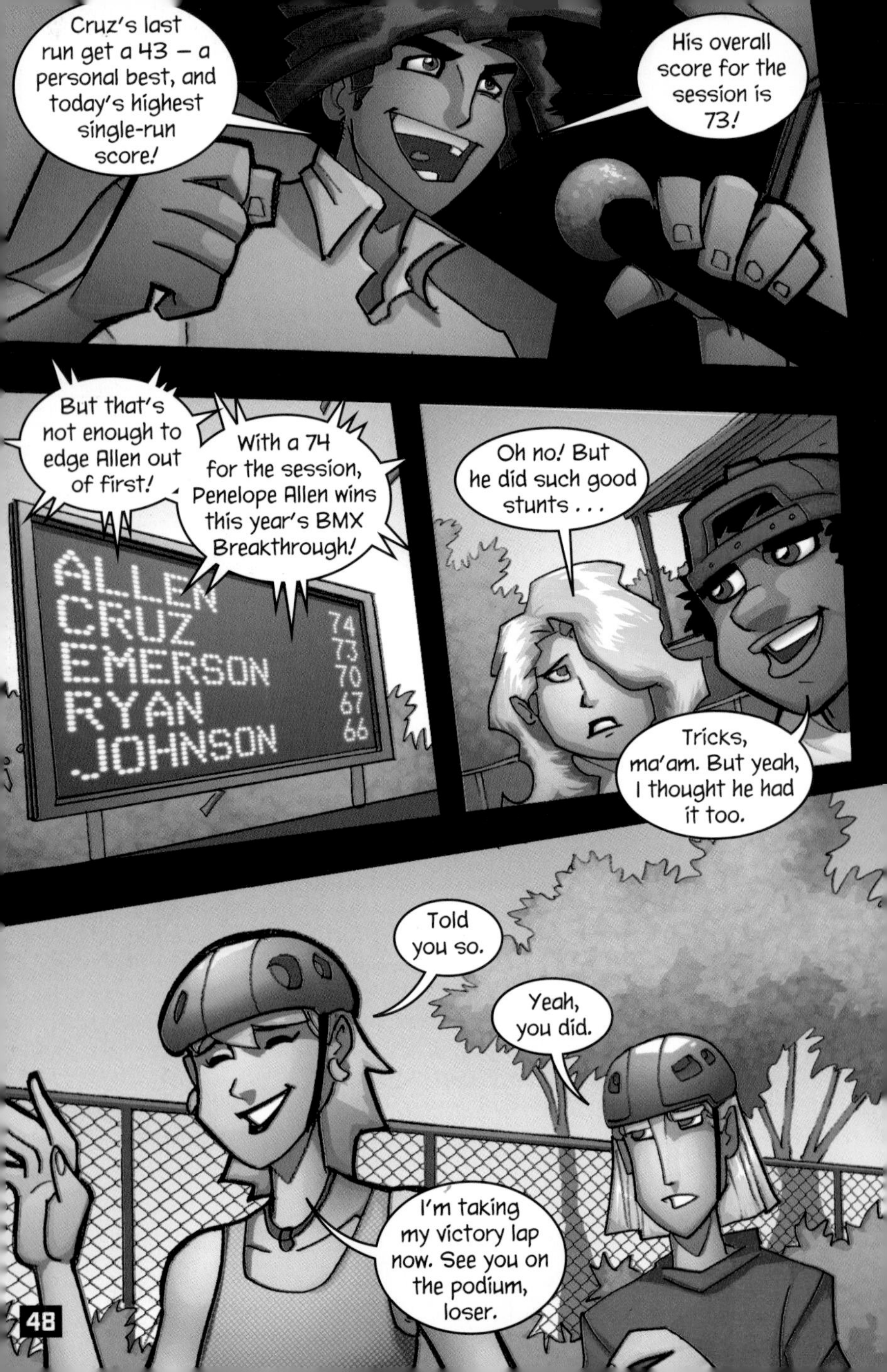
Cruz's last run get a 43 — a personal best, and today's highest single-run score!
His overall score for the session is 73!
But that's not enough to edge Allen out of first!
With a 74 for the session, Penelope Allen wins this year's BMX Breakthrough!
ALLEN 74
CRUZ 73
EMERSON 70
RYAN 67
JOHNSON 66
Oh no! But he did such good stunts . . .
Tricks, ma'am. But yeah, I thought he had it too.
Told you so.
Yeah, you did.
I'm taking my victory lap now. See you on the podium, loser.

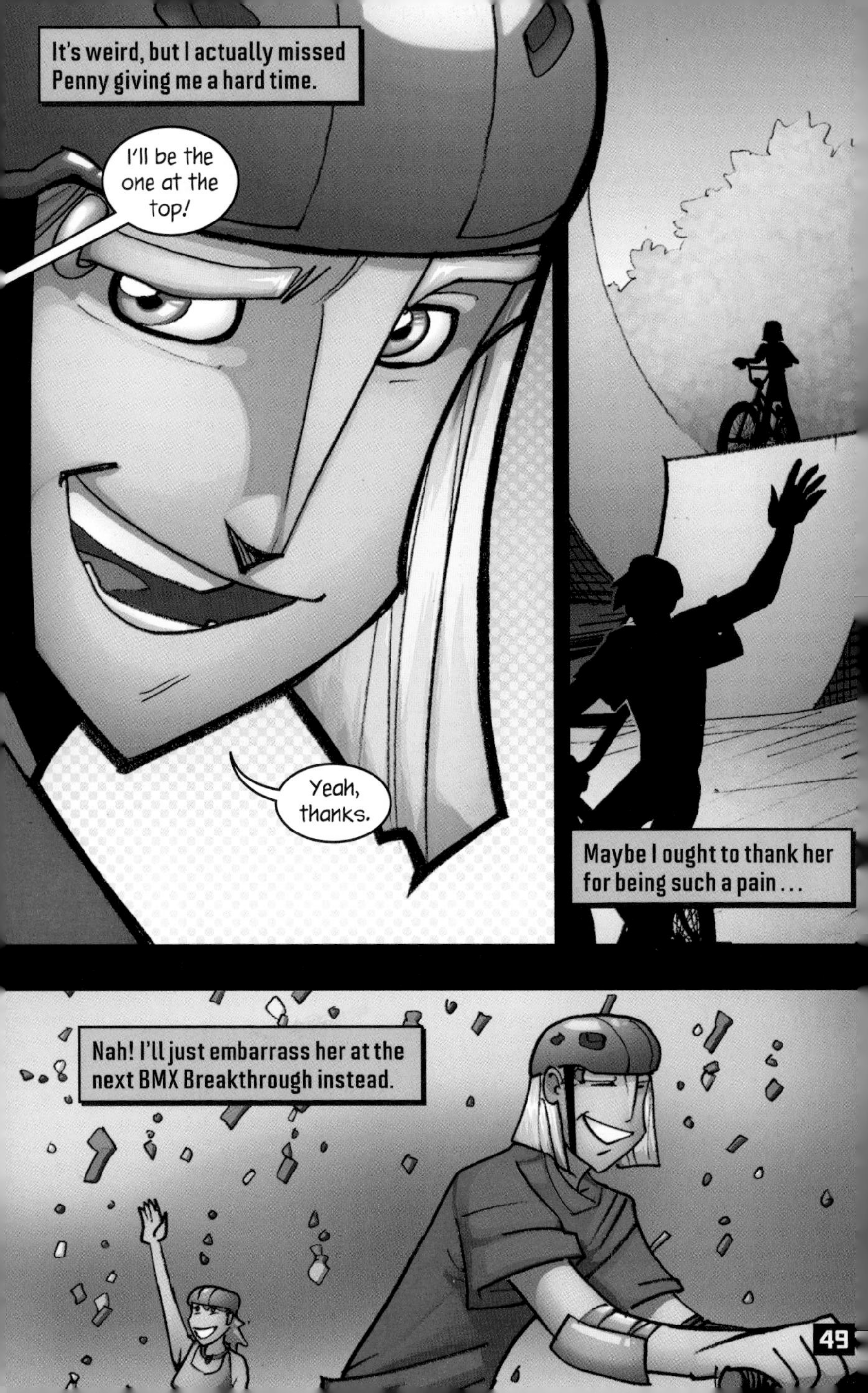
It's weird, but I actually missed Penny giving me a hard time.
I'll be the one at the top!
Yeah, thanks.
Maybe I ought to thank her for being such a pain...
Nah! I'll just embarrass her at the next BMX Breakthrough instead.

SPORTS ZONE

STGAME RECAP

MX
ESTYLE

PENNY ALLEN EDGES OUT BILL CRUZ FOR FIRST PLACE

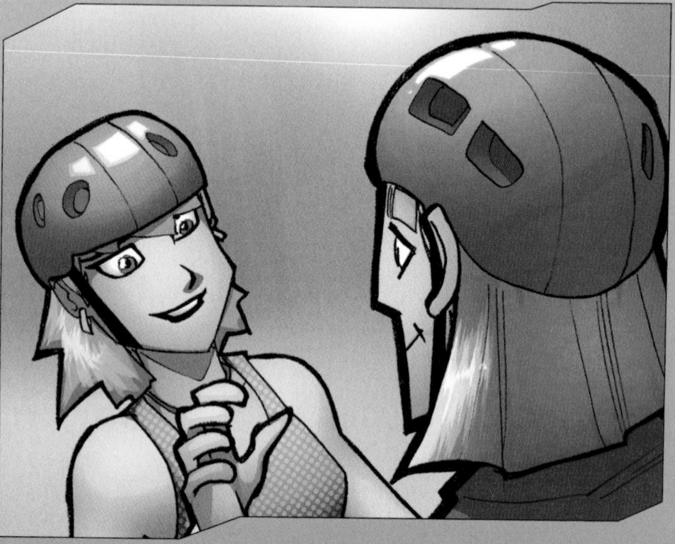

STORY: In a heated BMX battle, Penny managed to beat Bill by a single point in this year's BMX Breakthrough. After struggling with her first few runs, Penny picked up the pace and wowed the crowd with a creative array of tricks. Not to be outdone, Bill Cruz followed up with an even more impressive run — but Penny's cumulative total was still big enough to beat Bill — barely.

Y THE UMBERS

ST SCORES:
NGLE RUN: CRUZ, 43
ERALL: ALLEN, 74

Sports Illustrated KIDS

UP NEXT: SI KIDS INFO CENTER

SZ POSTGAME EXTRA

WHERE *YOU* ANALYZE THE GAME!

BLZ vs BNS
3-1

TGR vs ROR
33-32

EAG vs BAN
14-7

SPA vs WLD
4-3

BAN vs ROR
21-15

ROR vs UG
4-3

BLZ vs BNS
3-1

BMX fans got a real treat today when Penny Allen faced off against Bill Cruz in a memorable BMX battle. Let's go into the stands and ask some fans for their thoughts on the day's big event...

DISCUSSION QUESTION 1

Penny teases Bill about his BMX tricks. Can making fun of someone ever be a good thing? Why or why not?

DISCUSSION QUESTION 2

Bill's mom embarrasses him in front of his friends. Do your parents ever do anything that embarrasses you?

WRITING PROMPT 1

Bill was injured during a difficult trick attempt. Have you, or someone you know, ever gotten hurt playing a sport? Write about the experience.

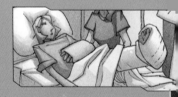

WRITING PROMPT 2

Design your own BMX trick. Write a basic summary of what your trick involves, then draw it in the comic-book style! Use several panels to show all the different steps of your amazing trick.

Sports Illustrated KIDS

INFO CENTER

GLOSSARY

BRILLIANT (BRIL-yuhnt)—spendid or amazing

CAN-CAN (KAN-KAN)—a midair trick where you kick one leg over t top tube of the bike, then put the foot back on the pedal.

DETERMINATION (di-tur-muh-NAY-shuhn)—firm desire to do something

DISTRACTED (diss-TRAKT-id)—weakened your concentration

EGO (EE-goh)—sense of self-importance

FLAIR (FLAYR)—trick where the rider and bike do a backflip anc 180 at once, then land facing back away from the ramp

FREESTYLE (FREE-stile)—BMX style based on performing tricks

MOCK (MOK)—make fun of someone in an unpleasant way

PRESSURE (PRESH-ur)—a burden or strain, usually from expectation

TOOTHPICK (TOOTH-pik)—a trick where the rider hangs the rear end their bike over the opposite side of the rail or ledge they a grinding

REATORS

Carl Bowen › Author

Carl Bowen is a father, husband, writer and editor who lives in Lawrenceville, Georgia. He was born in Louisiana, lived briefly in England, and was raised in Georgia, where he went to school. He has published a handful of novels, short stories, and comics. For Stone Arch, he has retold *20,000 Leagues Under the Sea*, *The Strange Case of Dr. Jekyll and Mr. Hyde*, *The Jungle Book*, "Aladdin and the Magic Lamp," *Julius Caesar*, and is working on *The Murders in the Rue Morgue*.

BMX Breakthrough is his first original graphic novel.

Gerardo Sandoval › Illustrator

Gerardo Sandoval is a professional comic book illustrator from Mexico. He has worked on many well-known comics including Tomb Raider books from Top Cow Production. He has also worked on designs for posters and card sets.

Benny Fuentes › Colorist

Benny Fuentes lives in Villahermosa, Tabasco in Mexico, where the temperature is just as hot as the sauce. He studied graphic design in college, but now he works as a full-time colorist in the comic book and graphic novel industry for companies like Marvel, DC Comics, and Top Cow Productions. He shares his home with two crazy cats, Chelo and Kitty, who act like they own the place.

Sports Illustrated KIDS GRAPHIC NOVELS

QUICK COMIC

HOUSTON MORIKAMI, PETER HILDEBRAND, and LUKE LAWLESS IN: **BMX BLITZ**

Excuse me, Pete?
What do you mean, "in person"?
Nothing.
What are you hiding, Hildebrand?
Heads up, Lawless.
Whoa!
No way!
SPLISH!
SPLISH!
SPLISH!

LOVE THIS QUICK COMIC? READ THE WHOLE STORY IN BMX BLITZ – ONLY FROM STONE ARCH BOOKS!

HOT SPORTS. HOT FORMAT!

GREAT CHARACTERS BATTLE FOR SPORTS GLORY IN TODAY'S HOTTEST FORMAT—GRAPHIC NOVELS!

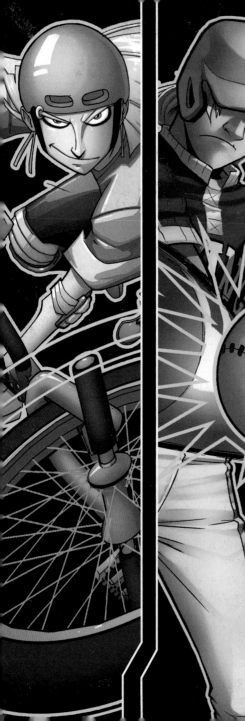
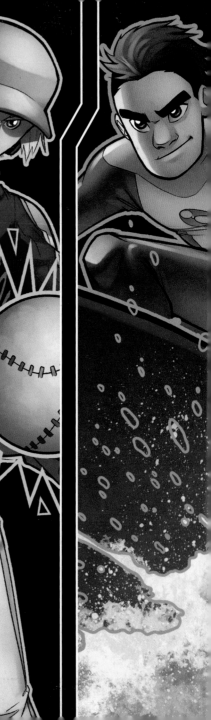